Zinc ALLOY

COLDFINGER

STONE ARCH BOOKS
MINNEAPOLIS   SAN DIEGO

Zinc ALLOY
COLDFINGER

WRITTEN BY **DONALD LEMKE**
ILLUSTRATED BY **DOUGLAS HOLGATE**

DESIGNER: **BRANN GARVEY**   ART DIRECTOR: **BOB LENTZ**

SERIES EDITOR: **DONALD LEMKE**   CREATIVE DIRECTOR: **HEATHER KINDSETH**

ASSOC. EDITOR: **SEAN TULIEN**   EDITORIAL DIRECTOR: **MICHAEL DAHL**

Graphic Sparks are published by Stone Arch Books, 151 Good Counsel Drive, P.O. Box 669, Mankato, Minnesota 56002
www.capstonepub.com Copyright © 2010 by Stone Arch Books. All rights reserved. No part of this publication may be reproduced in whole
or in part, or stored in a retrieval system, or transmitted in any form or by any means, electronic, mechanical, photocopying, recording, or
otherwise, without written permission of the publisher.

Library of Congress Cataloging-in-Publication Data
Lemke, Donald
 Coldfinger / by Donald Lemke ; illustrated by Douglas Holgate.
   p. cm. – (Graphic sparks. Zinc alloy)
  ISBN 978-1-4342-1586-4 (library binding)
  ISBN 978-1-4342-2314-2 (pbk.)
 1. Graphic novels. 2. Graphic novels. [1. Graphic novels. 2. Superheroes–Fiction. 3. Robots–Fiction. 4. Ski resorts–Fiction.] I.
Holgate, Douglas, ill. II. Title.
 PZ7.7.L46Co 2010
  741.5'973–dc22   2009011409

Summary: It's winter vacation, and Zack Allen's family is headed to the mountains. When Zack arrives, Johnny, the school's biggest
bully, tricks him into entering the annual ski competition. While on the slopes, however, Zack discovers an even greater problem, an
evil villain is building a giant freeze ray within the mountain. Now Zinc must stop his evil plans and take home the ski trophy.

Printed in the United States of America in Stevens Point, Wisconsin.
052010   005814R

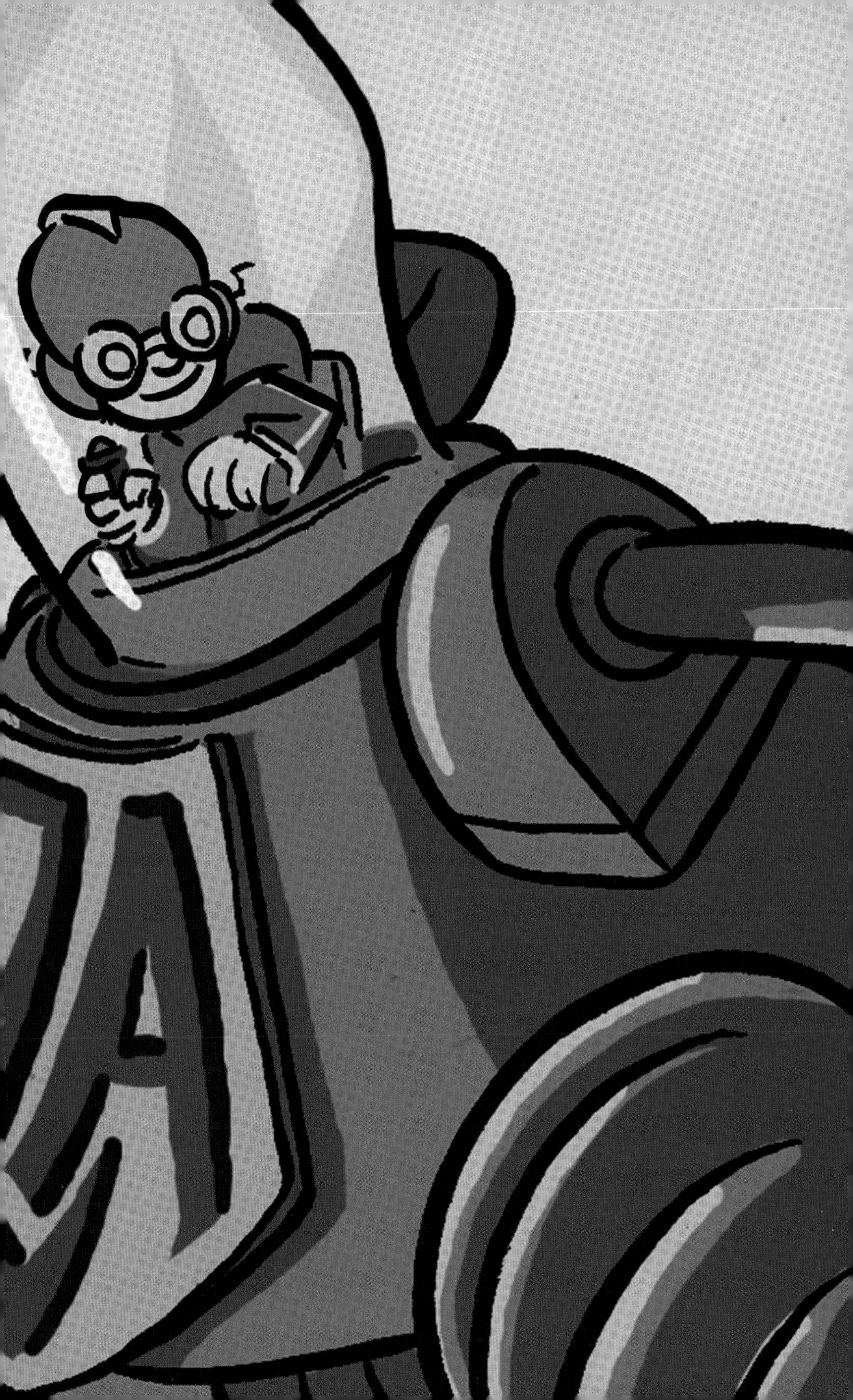

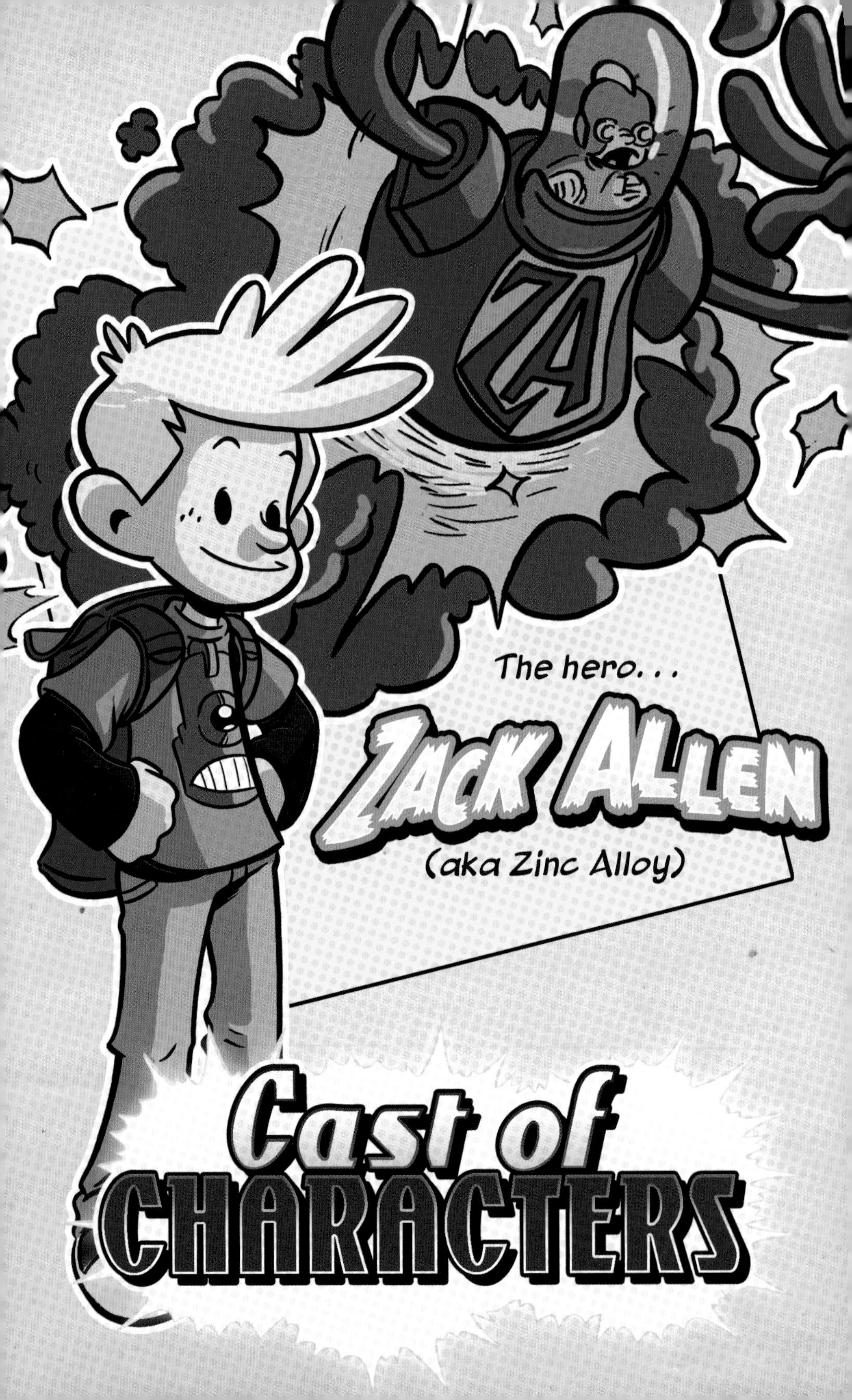

The hero...
ZACK ALLEN
(aka Zinc Alloy)
Cast of
CHARACTERS

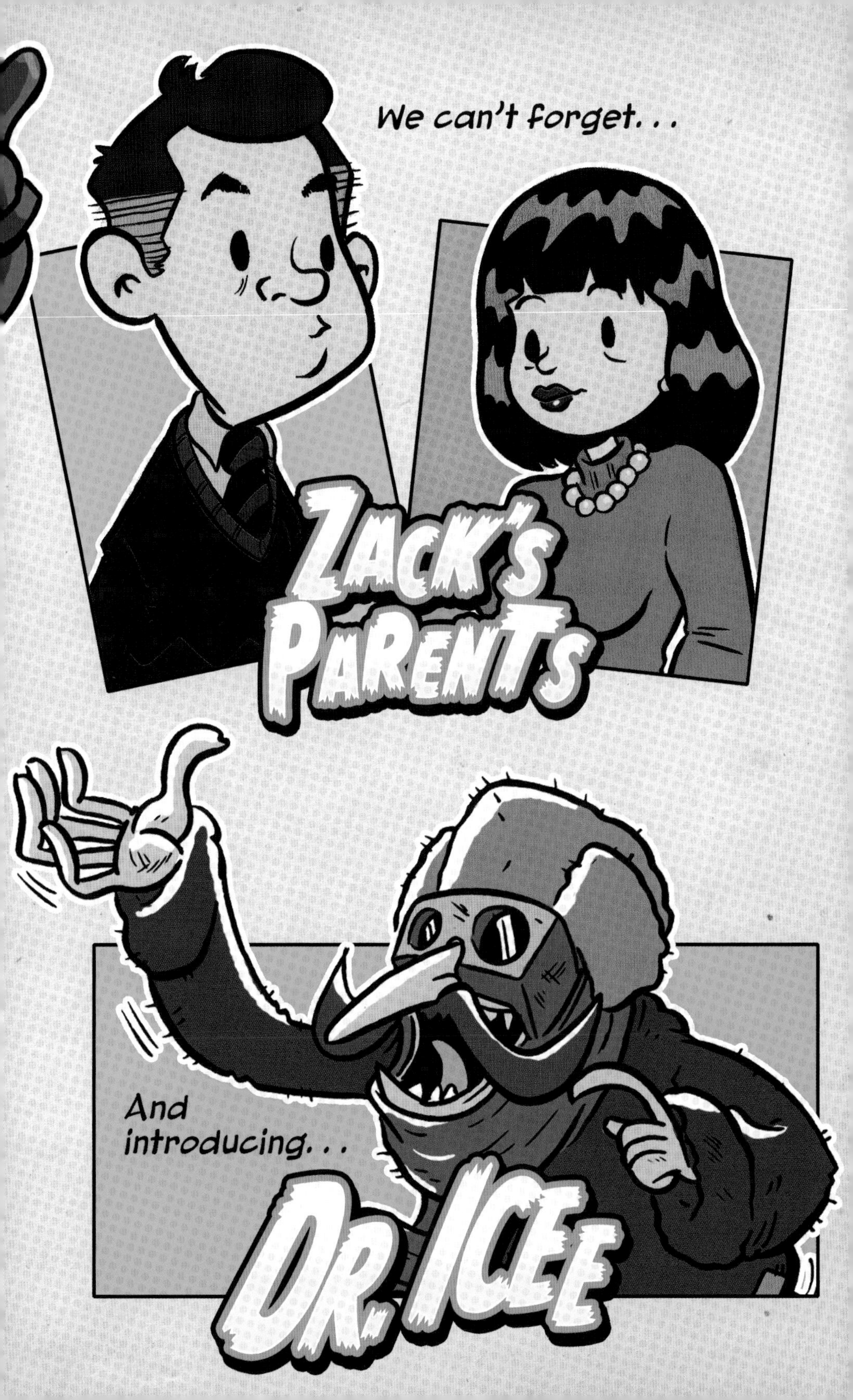
We can't forget...
ZACK'S PARENTS
And introducing...
DR. ICEE

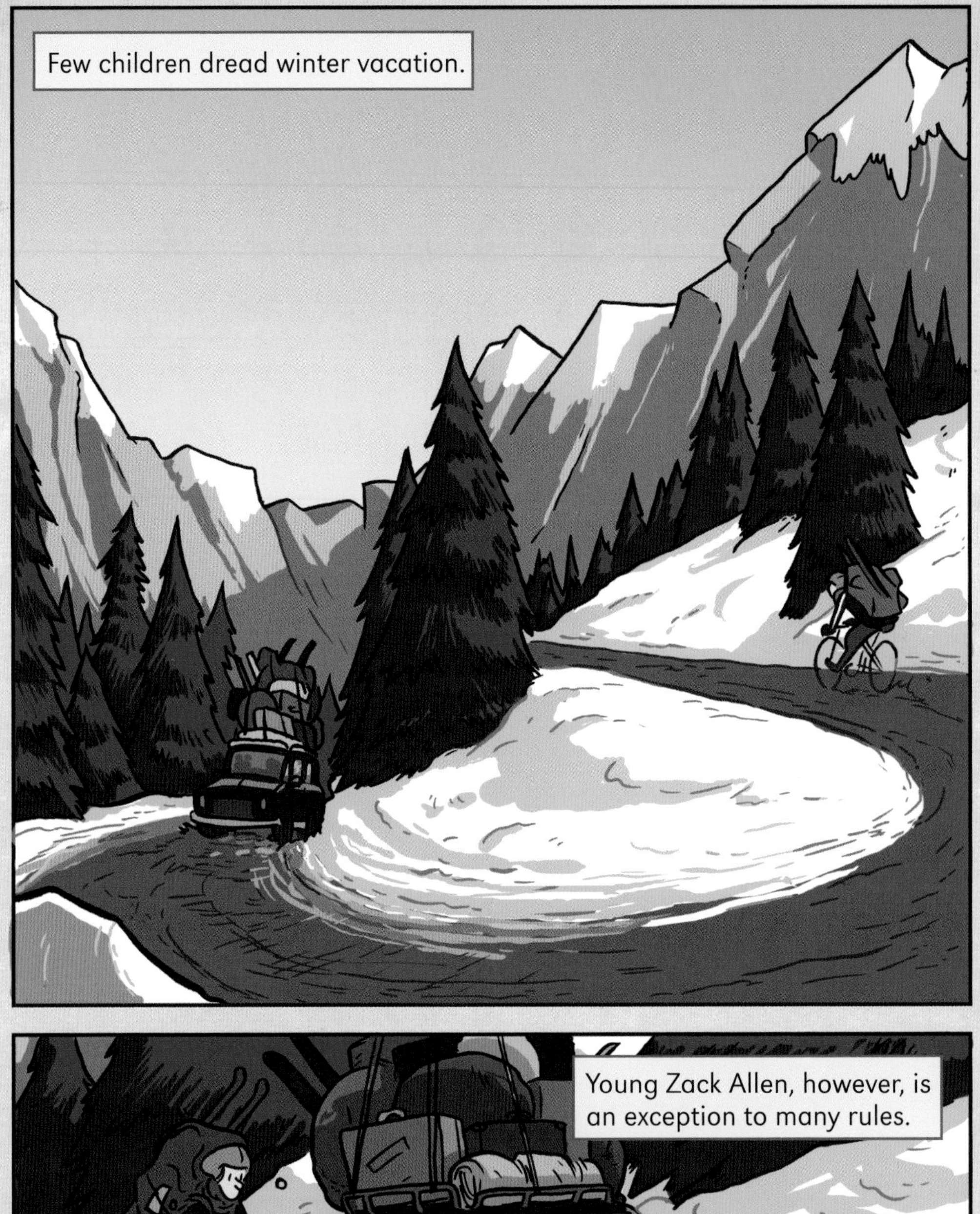
Few children dread winter vacation.

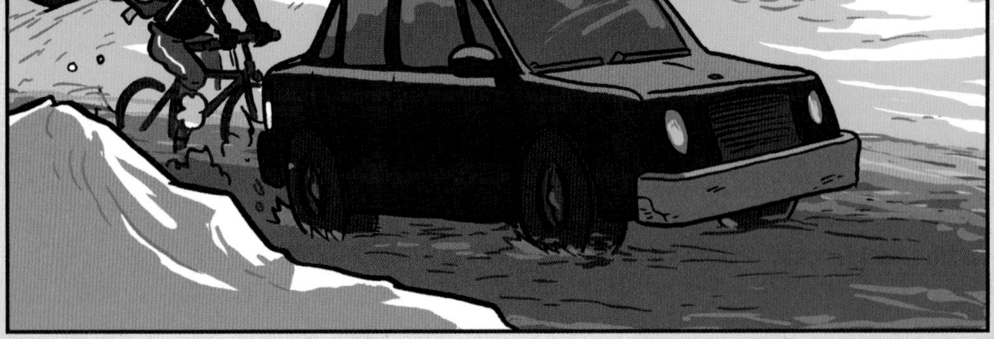
Young Zack Allen, however, is an exception to many rules.

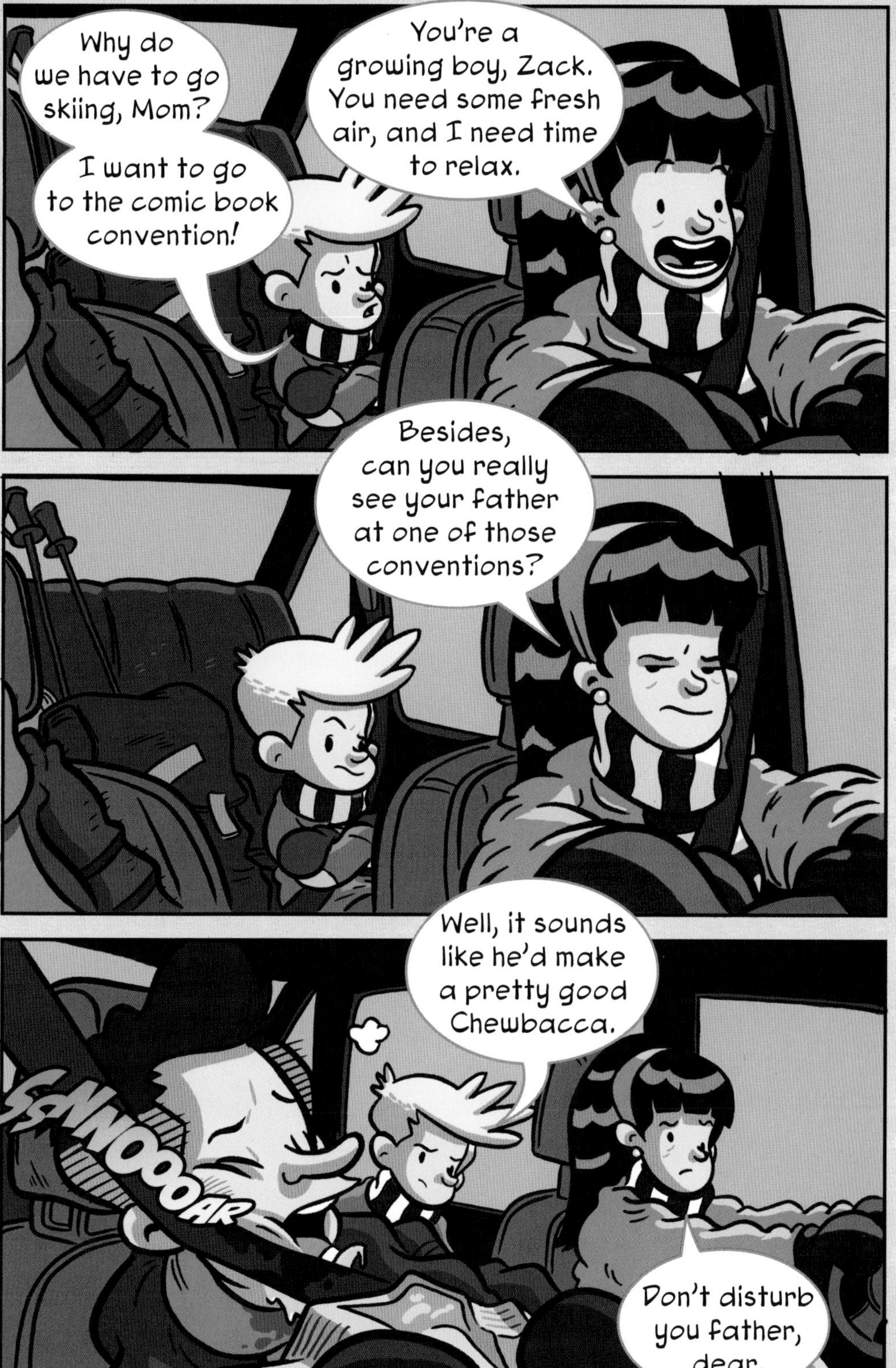
Why do we have to go skiing, Mom?
I want to go to the comic book convention!
You're a growing boy, Zack. You need some fresh air, and I need time to relax.
Besides, can you really see your father at one of those conventions?
Well, it sounds like he'd make a pretty good Chewbacca.
Don't disturb you father, dear.

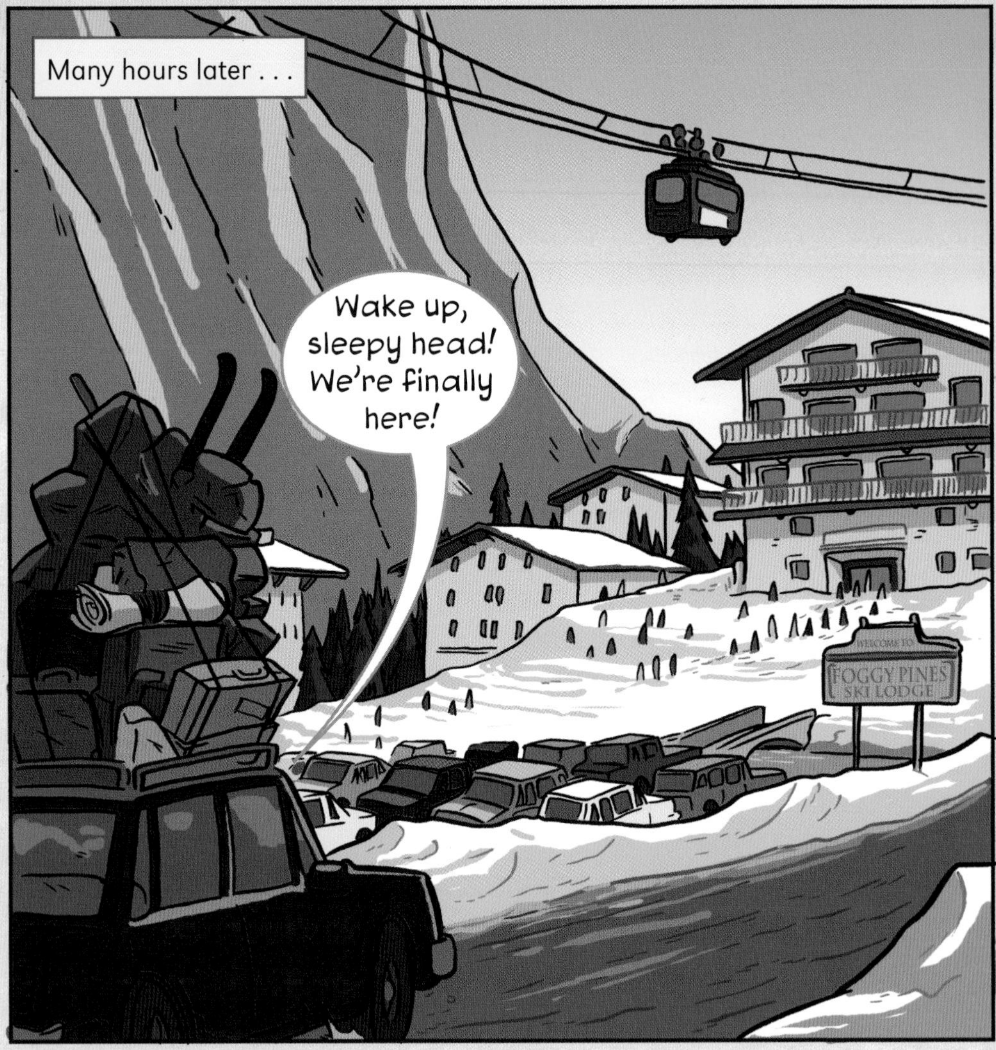
Many hours later . . .
Wake up, sleepy head! We're finally here!
WELCOME TO
FOGGY PINES SKI LODGE

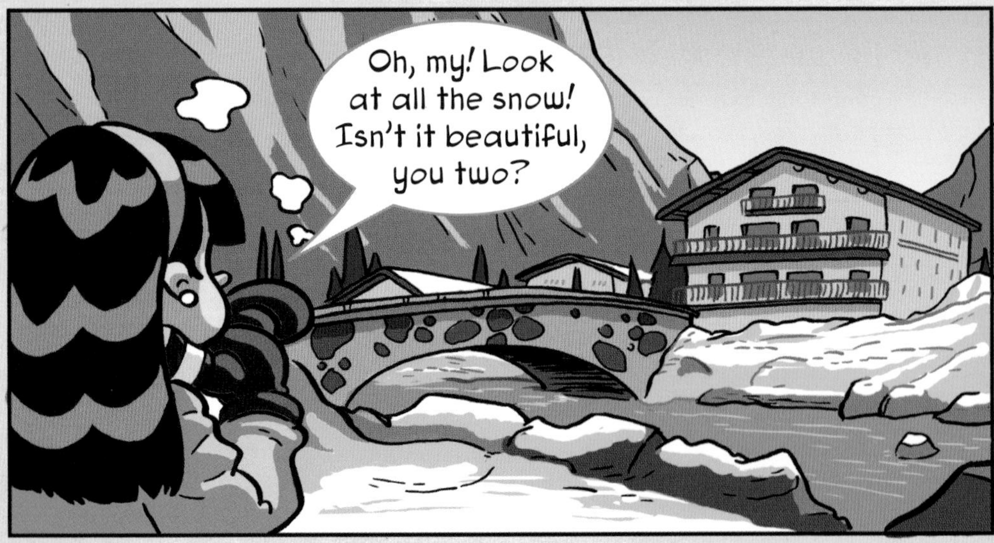
Oh, my! Look at all the snow! Isn't it beautiful, you two?

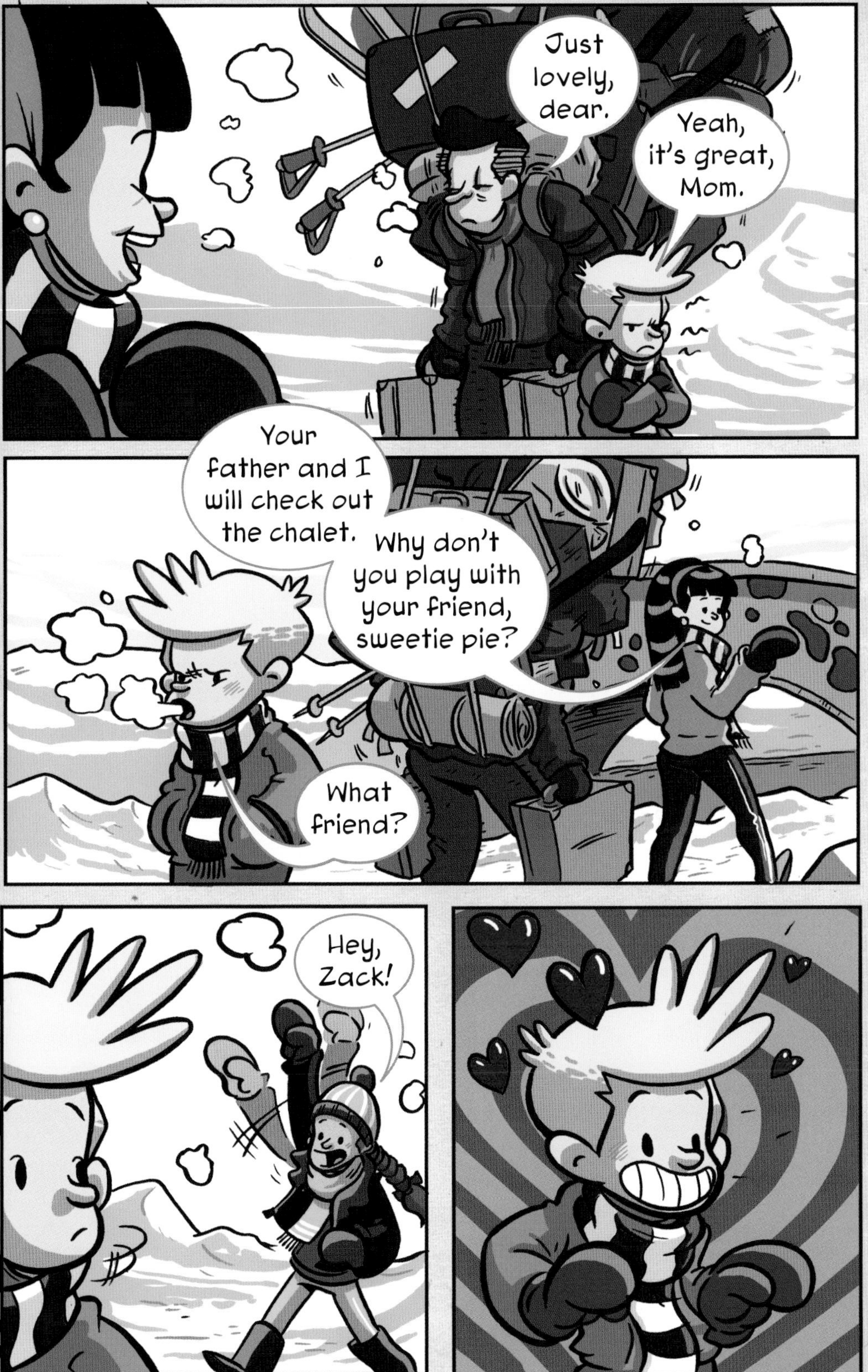
Just lovely, dear.
Yeah, it's great, Mom.
Your father and I will check out the chalet.
Why don't you play with your friend, sweetie pie?
What friend?
Hey, Zack!

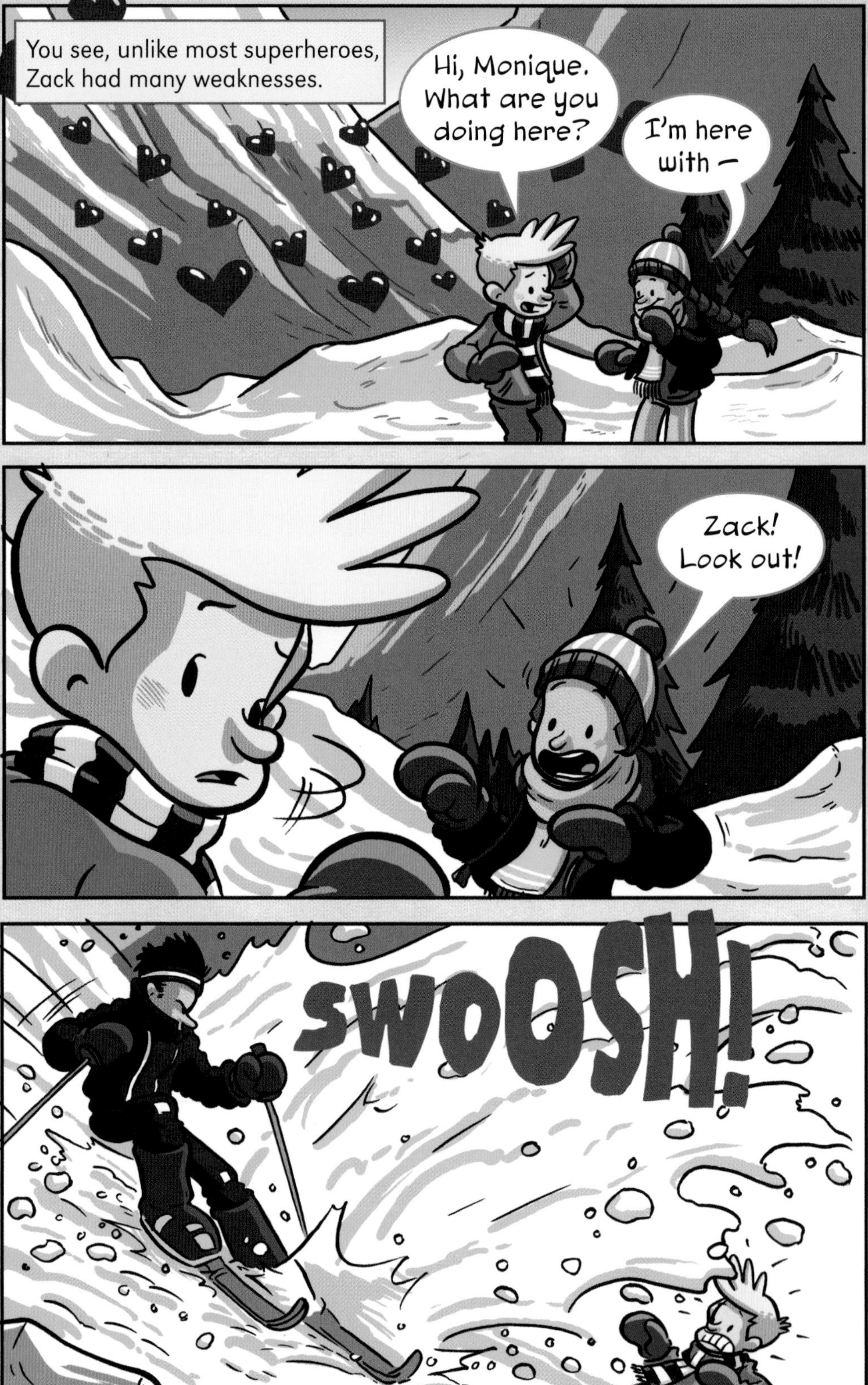
You see, unlike most superheroes, Zack had many weaknesses.
Hi, Monique. What are you doing here?
I'm here with —
Zack! Look out!
SWOOSH!

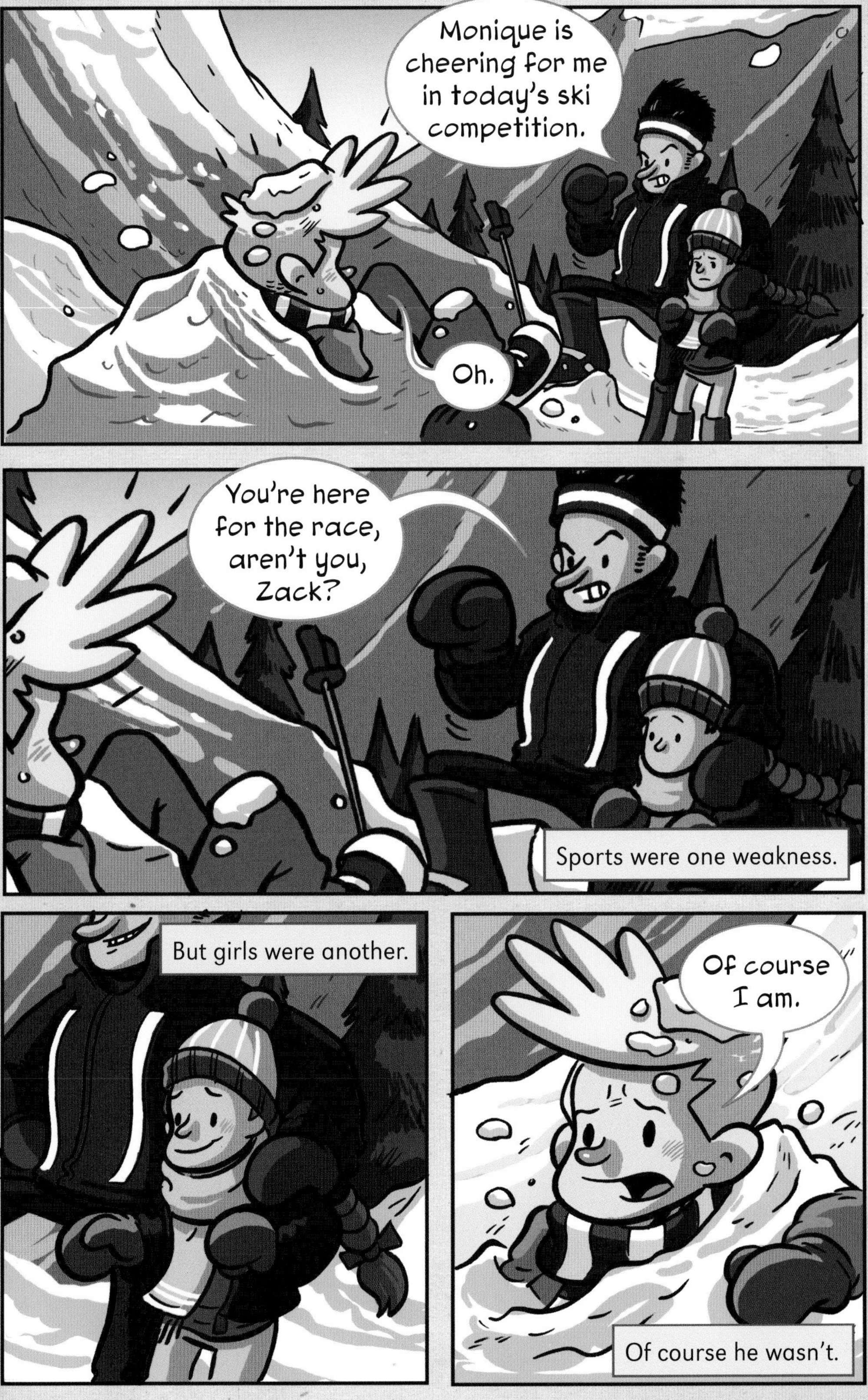
Monique is cheering for me in today's ski competition.
Oh.
You're here for the race, aren't you, Zack?
Sports were one weakness.
But girls were another.
Of course I am.
Of course he wasn't.

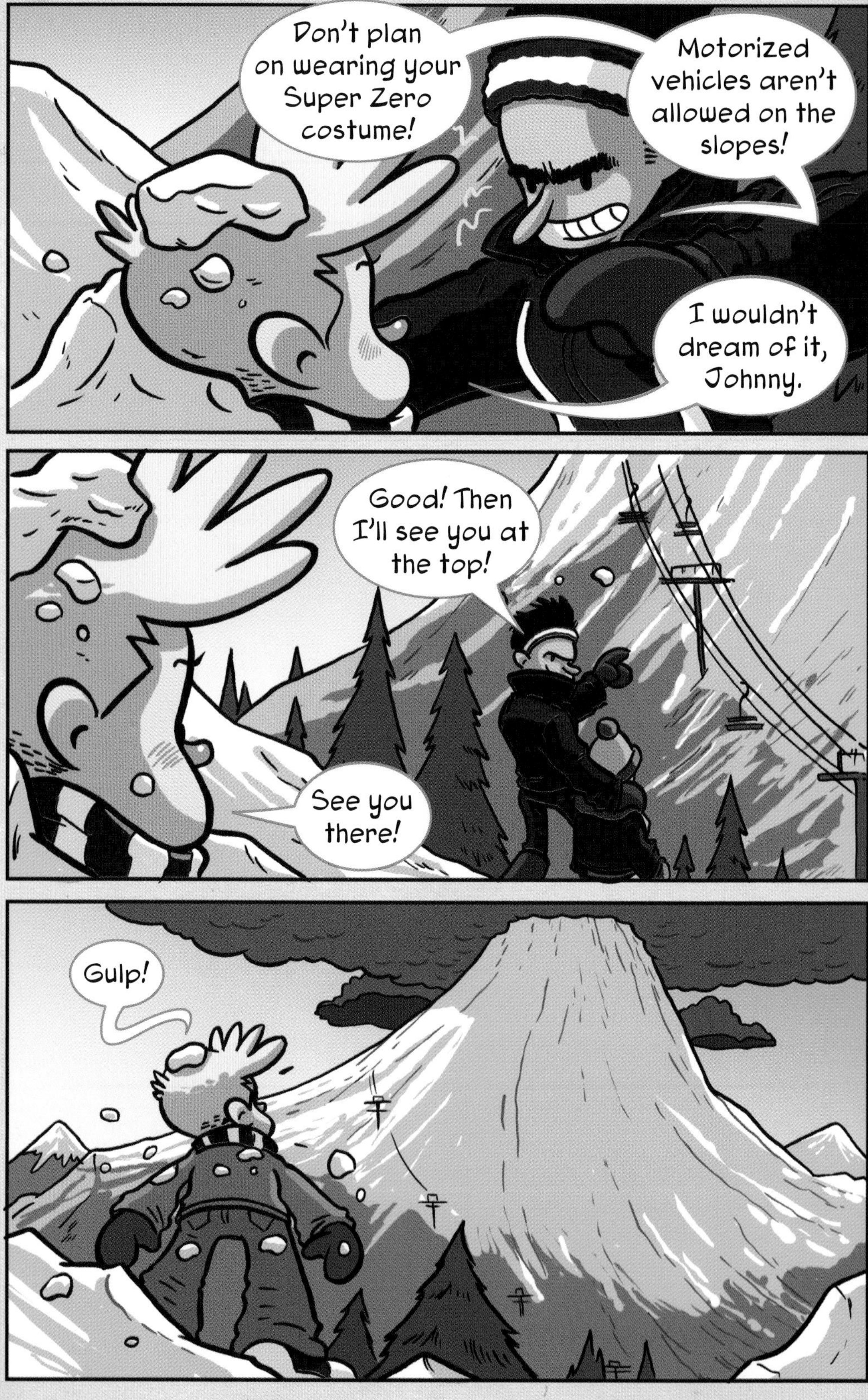
Don't plan on wearing your Super Zero costume!
Motorized vehicles aren't allowed on the slopes!
I wouldn't dream of it, Johnny.
Good! Then I'll see you at the top!
See you there!
Gulp!

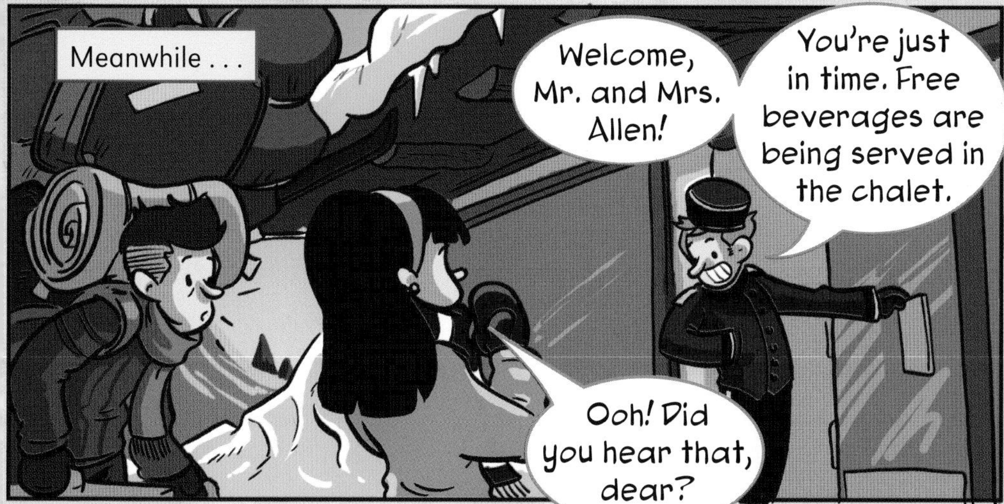
Meanwhile . . .
Welcome, Mr. and Mrs. Allen!
You're just in time. Free beverages are being served in the chalet.
Ooh! Did you hear that, dear?

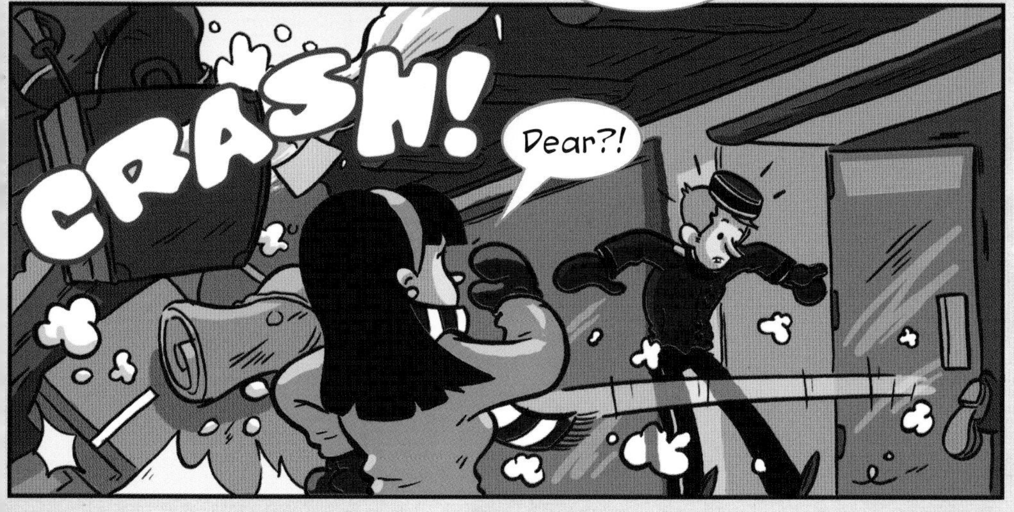
CRASH!
Dear?!

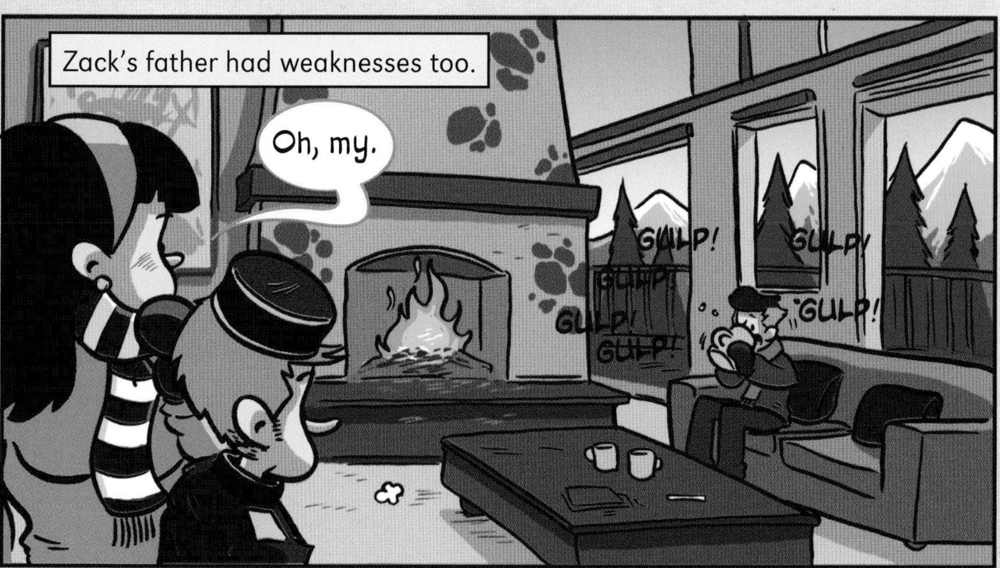
Zack's father had weaknesses too.
Oh, my.
GULP!
GULP!
GULP!
GULP!
GULP!
GULP!

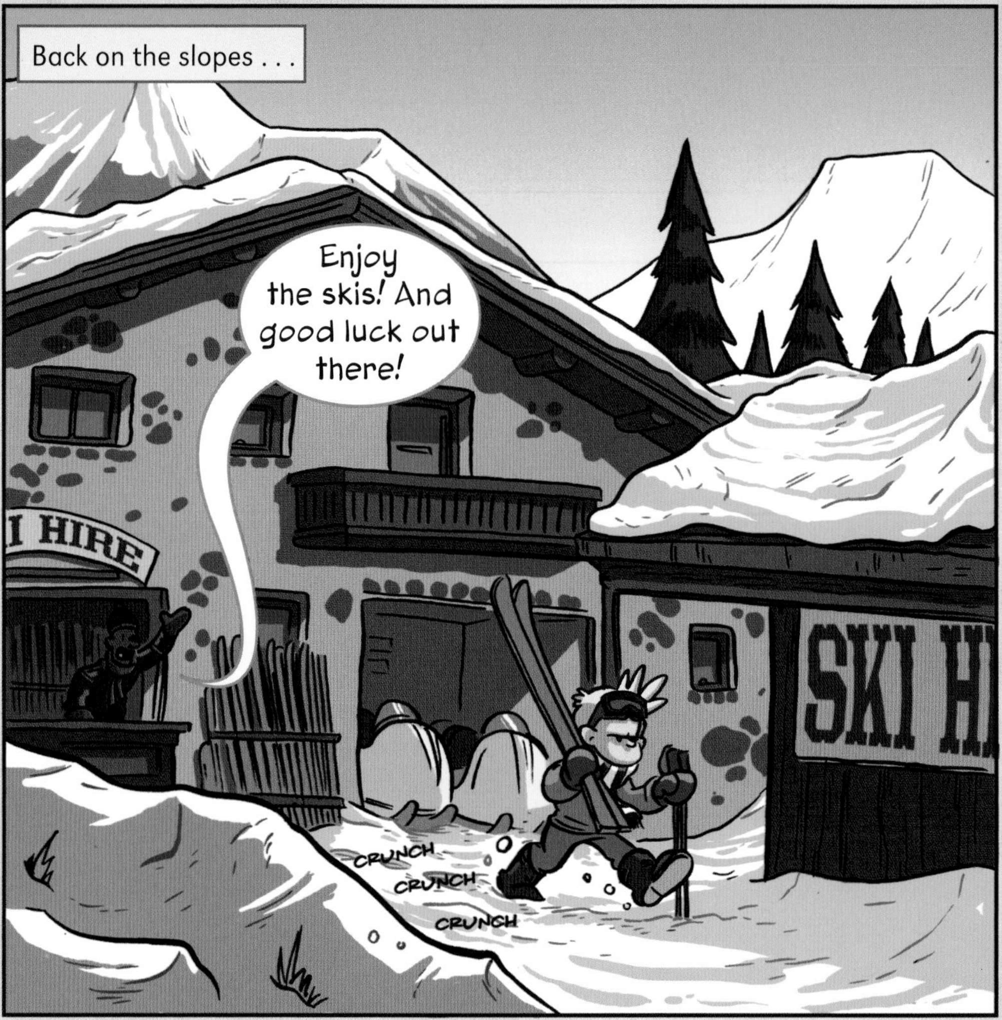
Back on the slopes . . .
Enjoy the skis! And good luck out there!
I HIRE
SKI H
CRUNCH
CRUNCH
CRUNCH

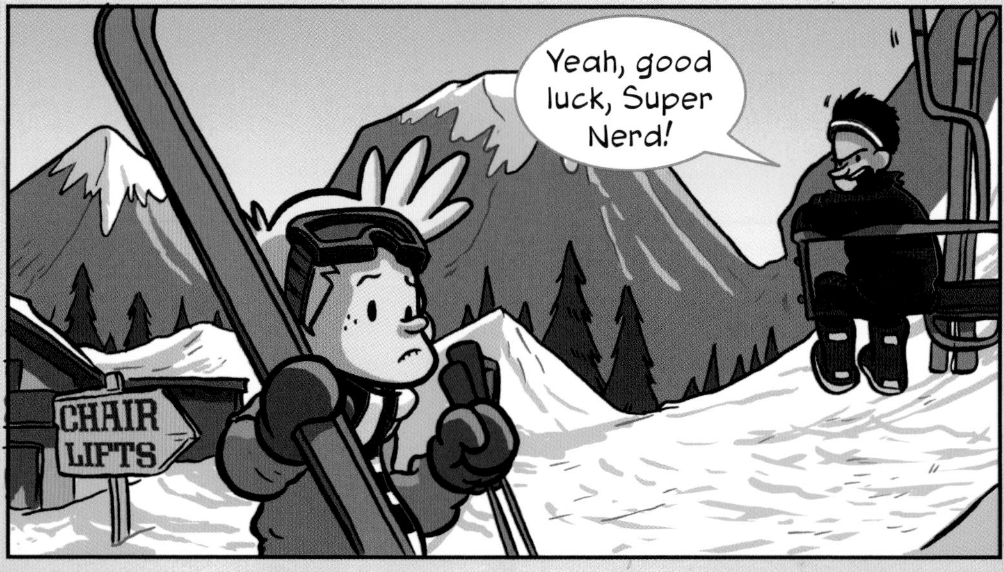
Yeah, good luck, Super Nerd!
CHAIR LIFTS

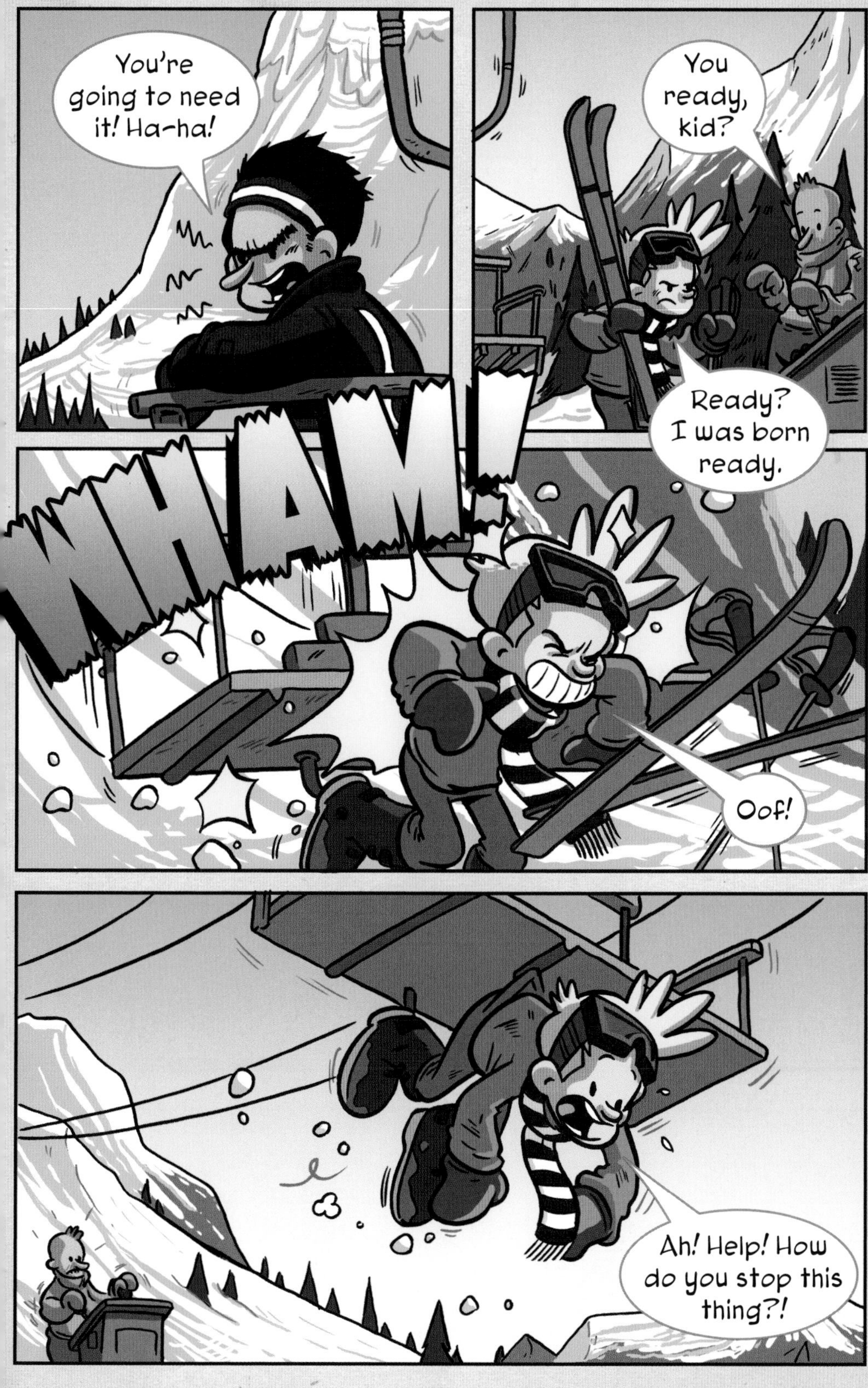
You're going to need it! Ha-ha!
You ready, kid?
Ready? I was born ready.
WHAM!
Oof!
Ah! Help! How do you stop this thing?!

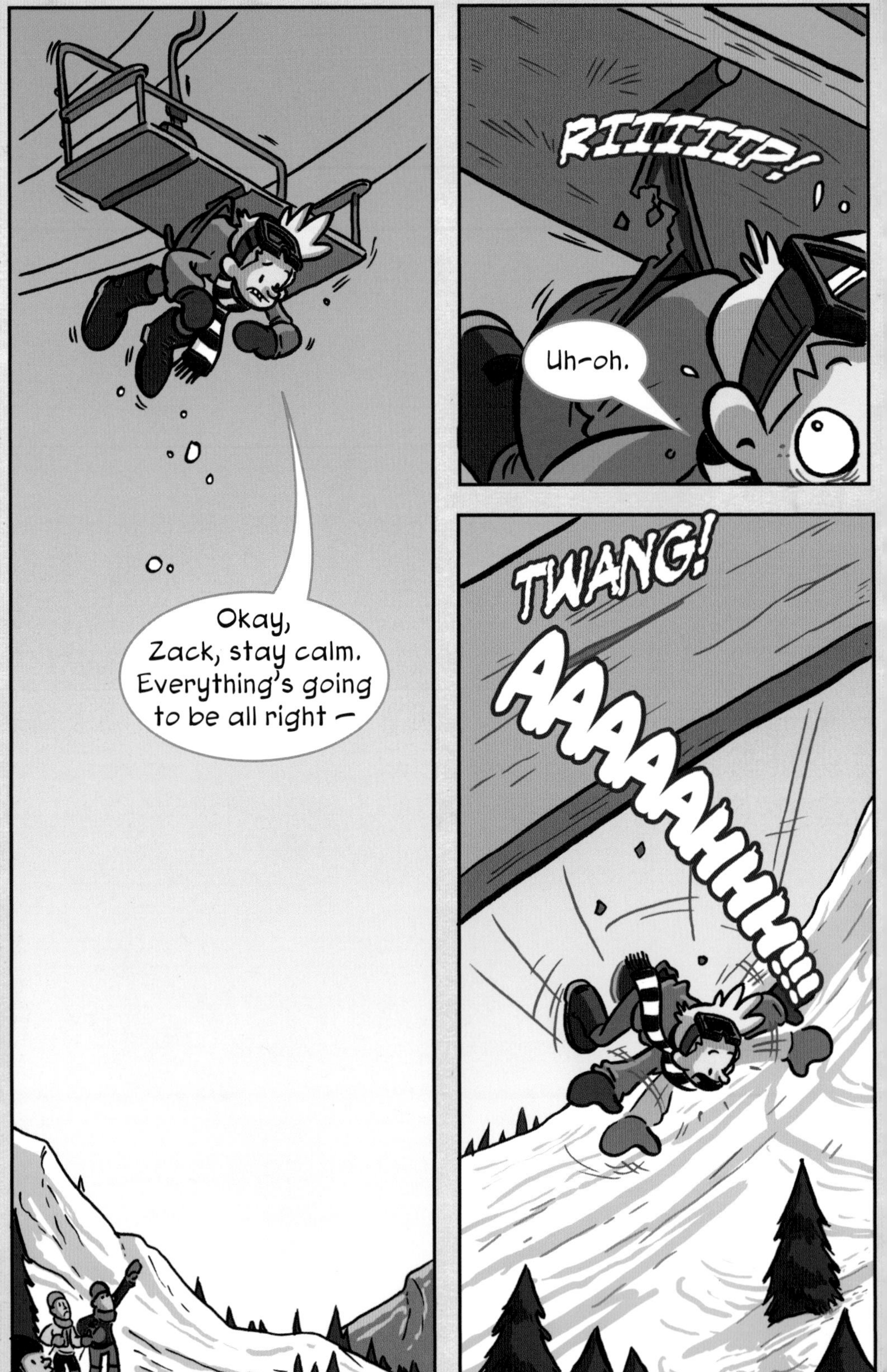
Okay,
Zack, stay calm.
Everything's going
to be all right —
RIIIIIP!
Uh-oh.
TWANG!
AAAAAHHH!!!

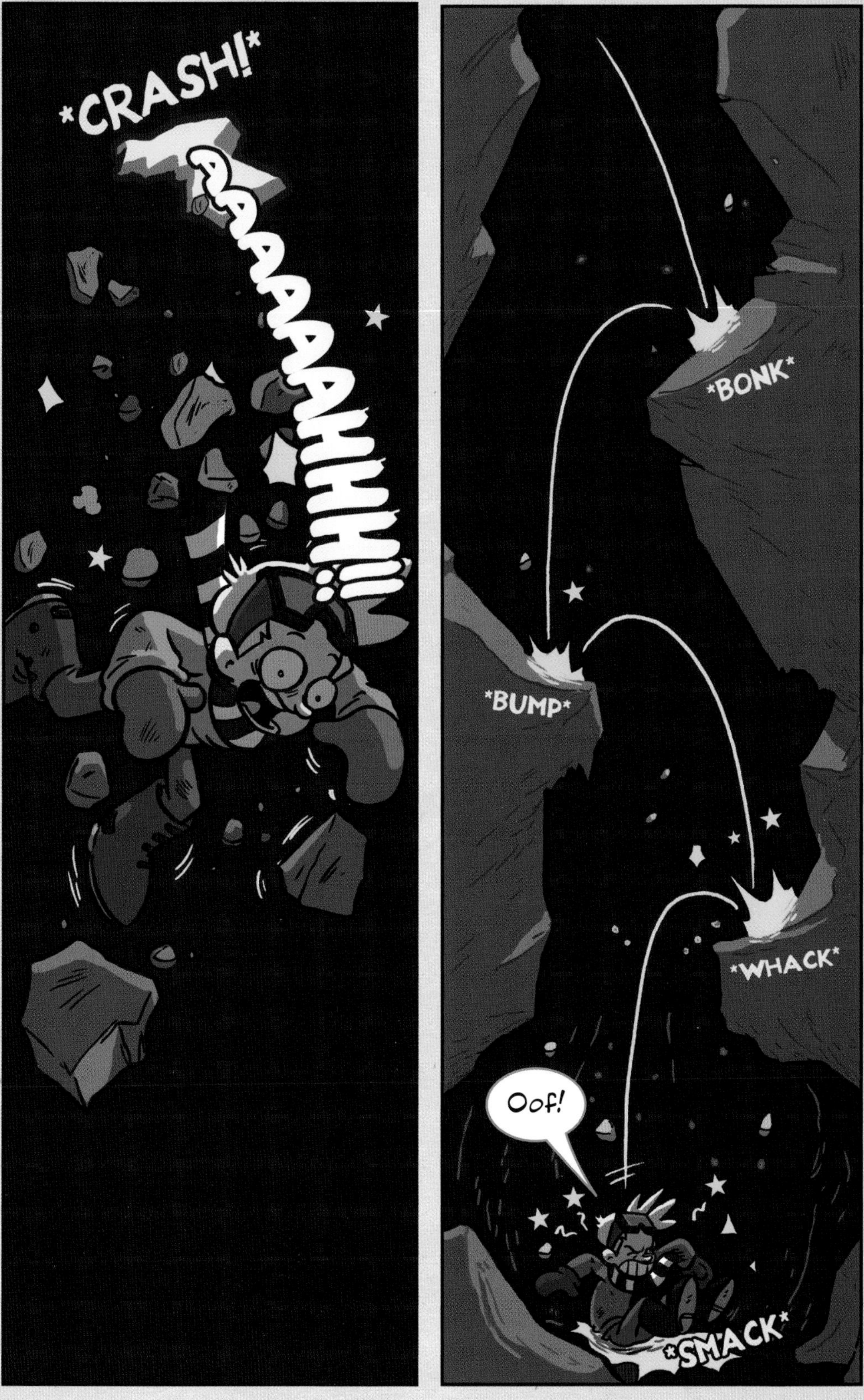
CRASH!
AAAAAAAHHHHH!!!
BONK
BUMP
WHACK
Oof!
SMACK

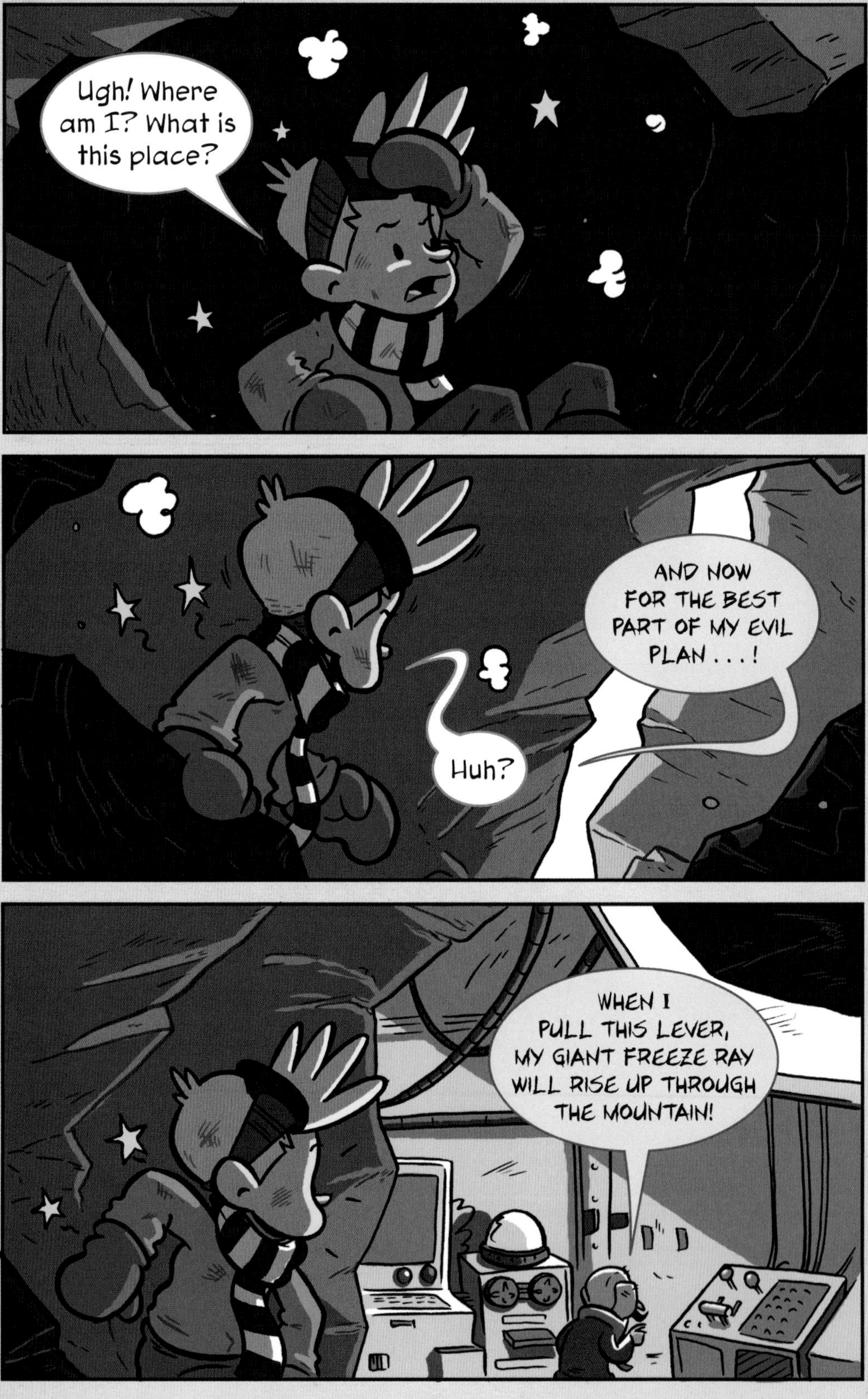
Ugh! Where am I? What is this place?
AND NOW FOR THE BEST PART OF MY EVIL PLAN . . . !
Huh?
WHEN I PULL THIS LEVER, MY GIANT FREEZE RAY WILL RISE UP THROUGH THE MOUNTAIN!

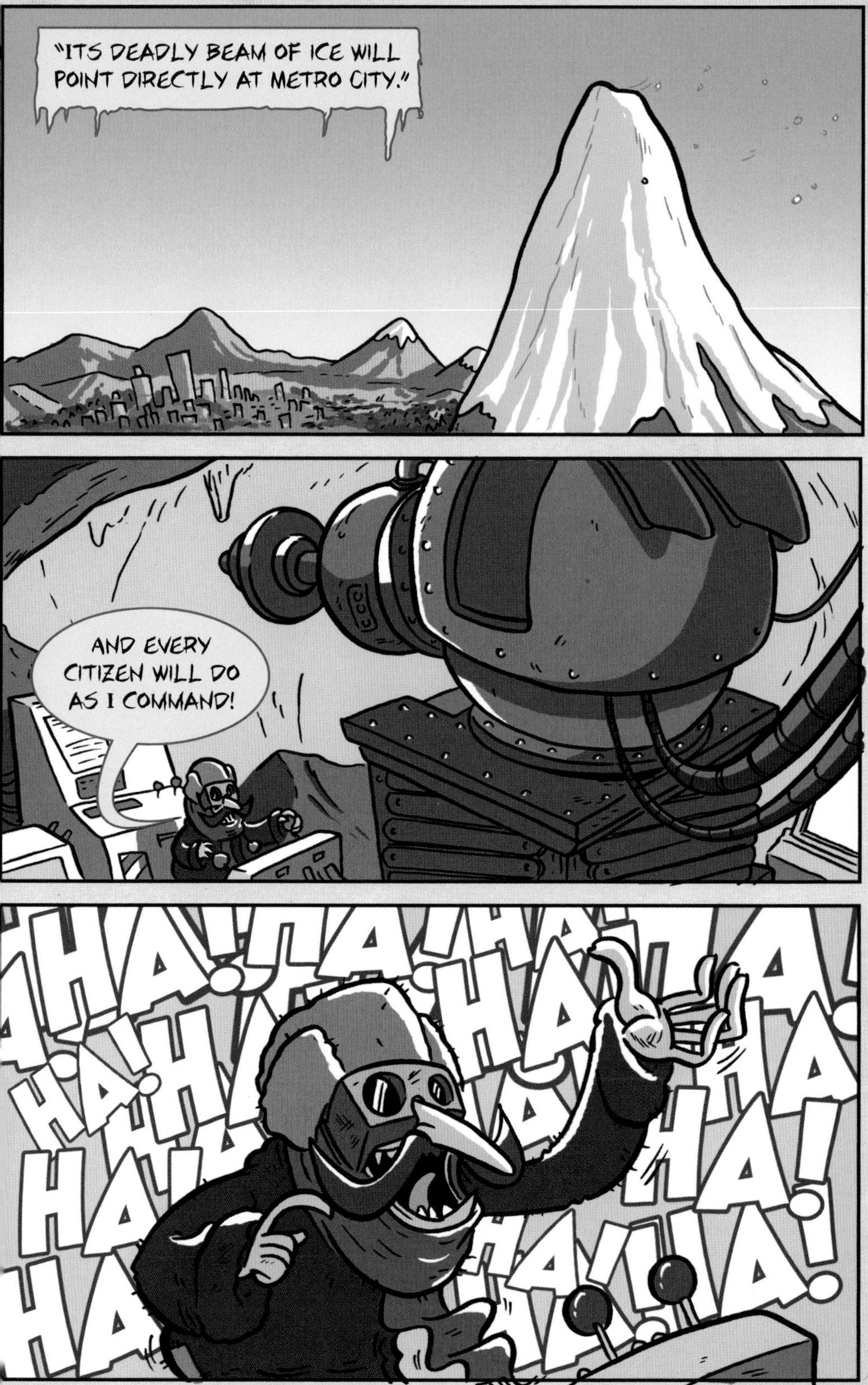
"ITS DEADLY BEAM OF ICE WILL POINT DIRECTLY AT METRO CITY."
AND EVERY CITIZEN WILL DO AS I COMMAND!
HA! HA! HA! HA! HA! HA! HA! HA! HA! HA! HA! HA! HA! HA!

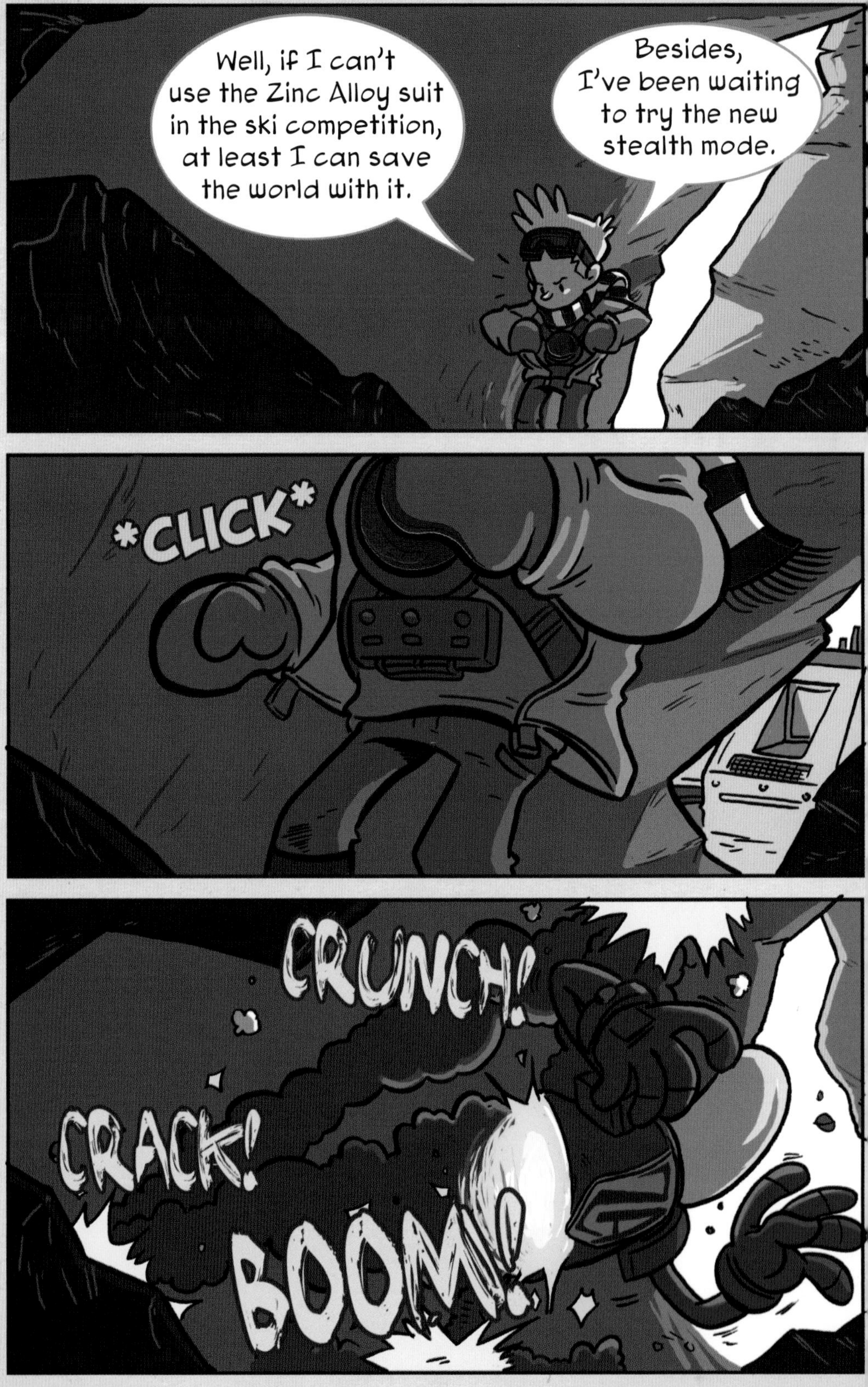
Well, if I can't use the Zinc Alloy suit in the ski competition, at least I can save the world with it.
Besides, I've been waiting to try the new stealth mode.
CLICK
CRUNCH!
CRACK!
BOOM!

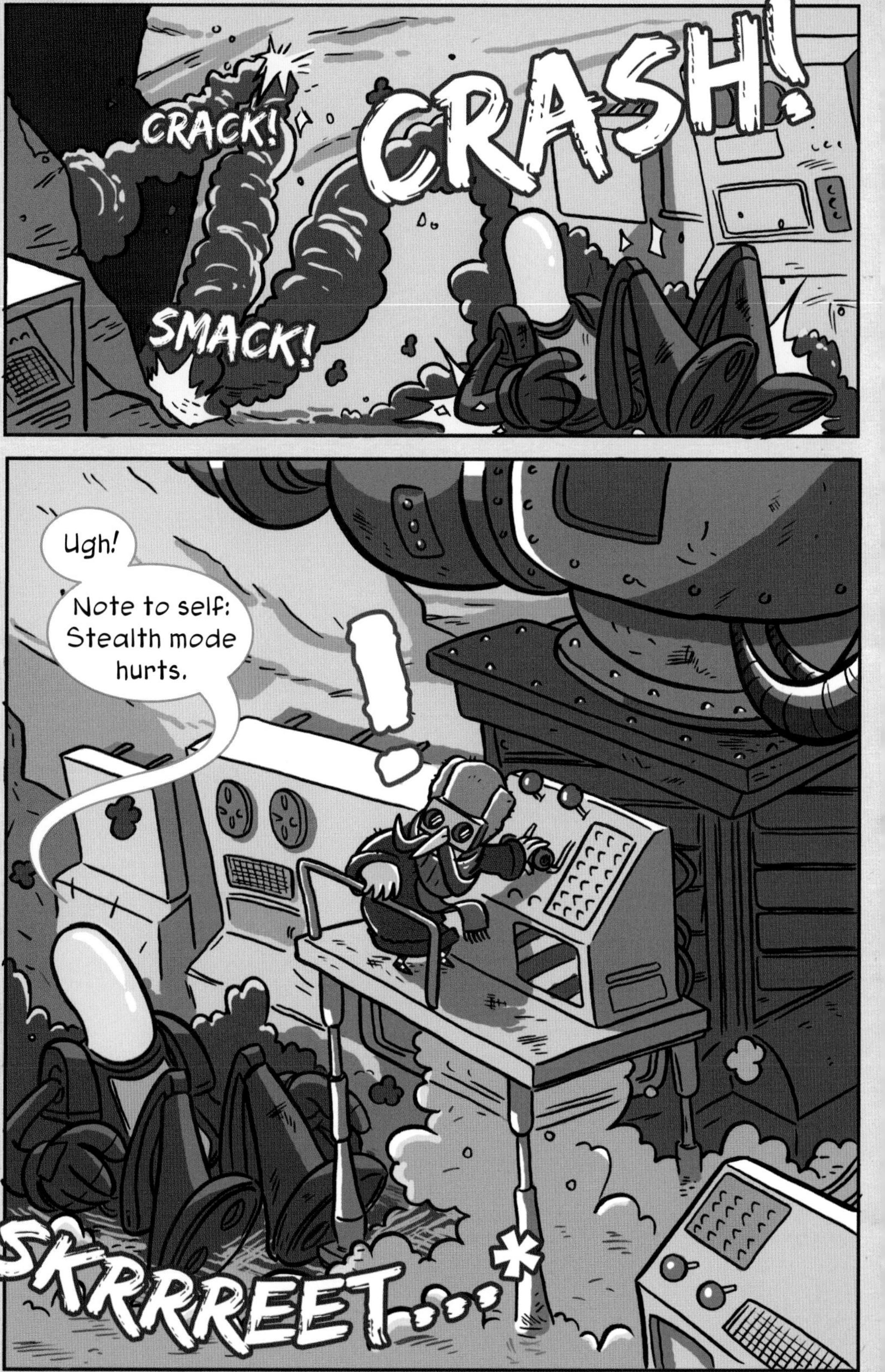
CRACK!
SMACK!
CRASH!
Ugh!
Note to self: Stealth mode hurts.
SKRRREET...!

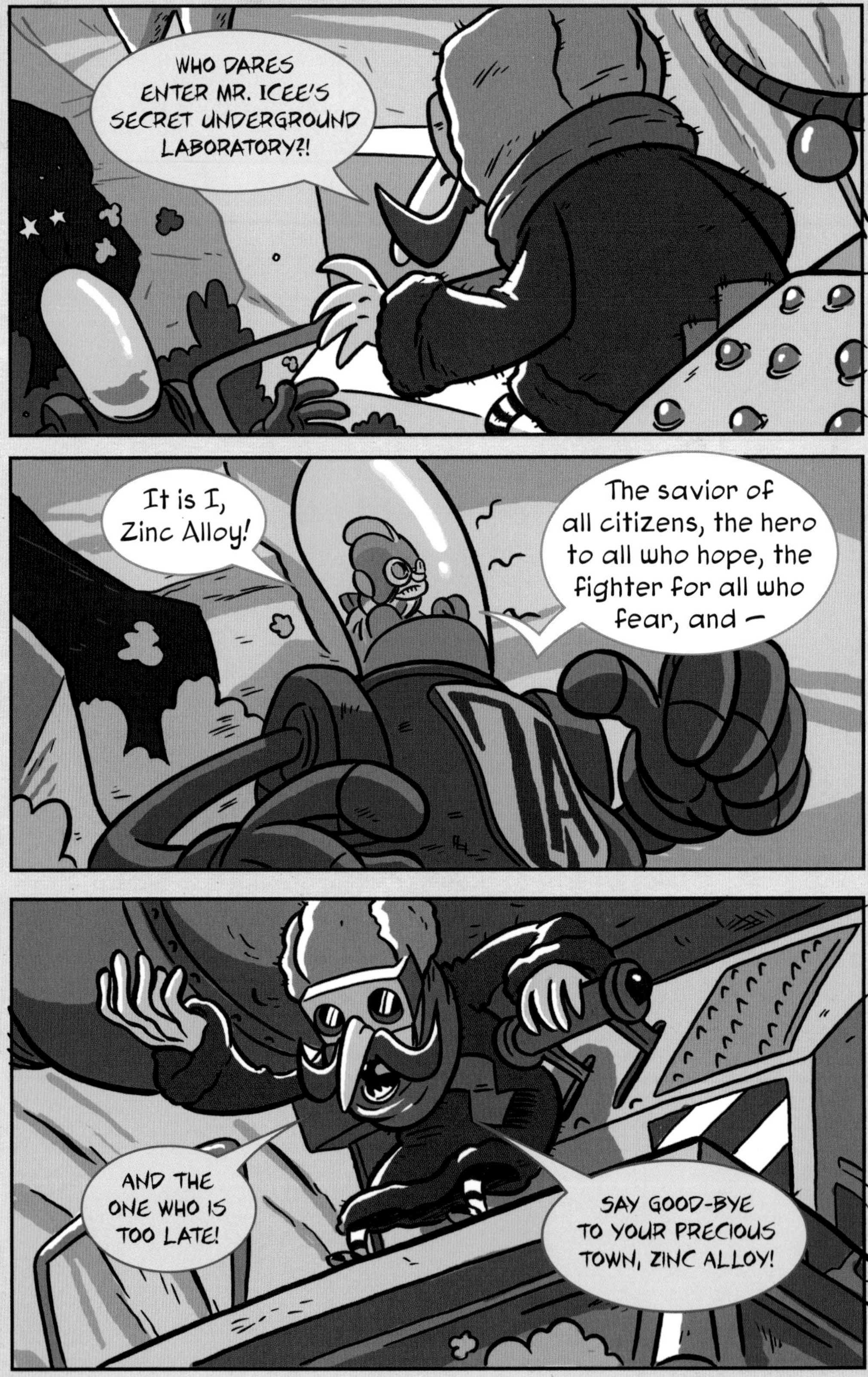
WHO DARES ENTER MR. ICEE'S SECRET UNDERGROUND LABORATORY?!
It is I, Zinc Alloy!
The savior of all citizens, the hero to all who hope, the fighter for all who fear, and —
AND THE ONE WHO IS TOO LATE!
SAY GOOD-BYE TO YOUR PRECIOUS TOWN, ZINC ALLOY!

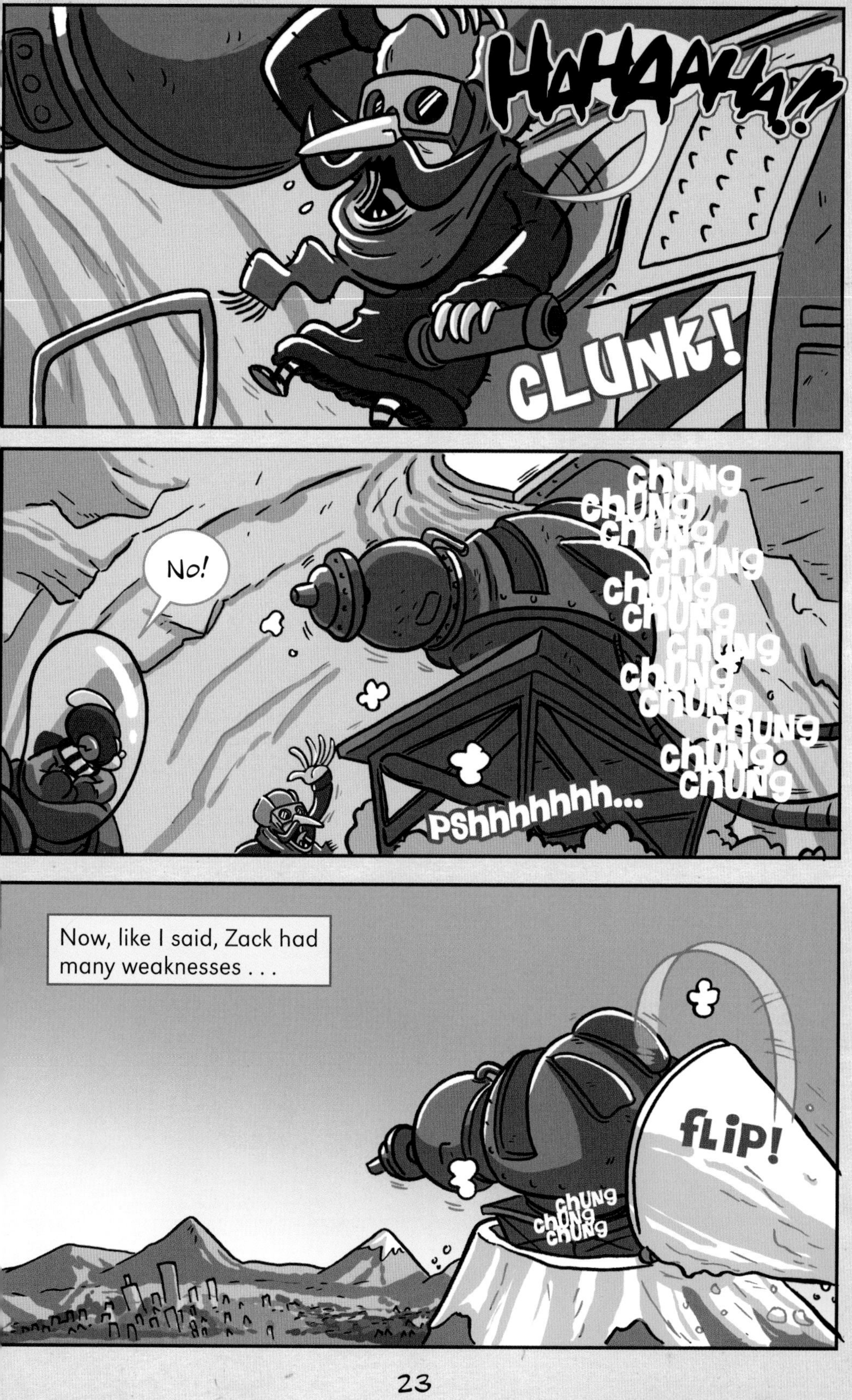
HAHAAHA!!
CLUNK!
No!
chung
chung
chung
chung
chung
chung
chung
chung
chung
chung
chung
chung
Pshhhhhhh...
Now, like I said, Zack had many weaknesses . . .
FLIP!
chung
chung
chung

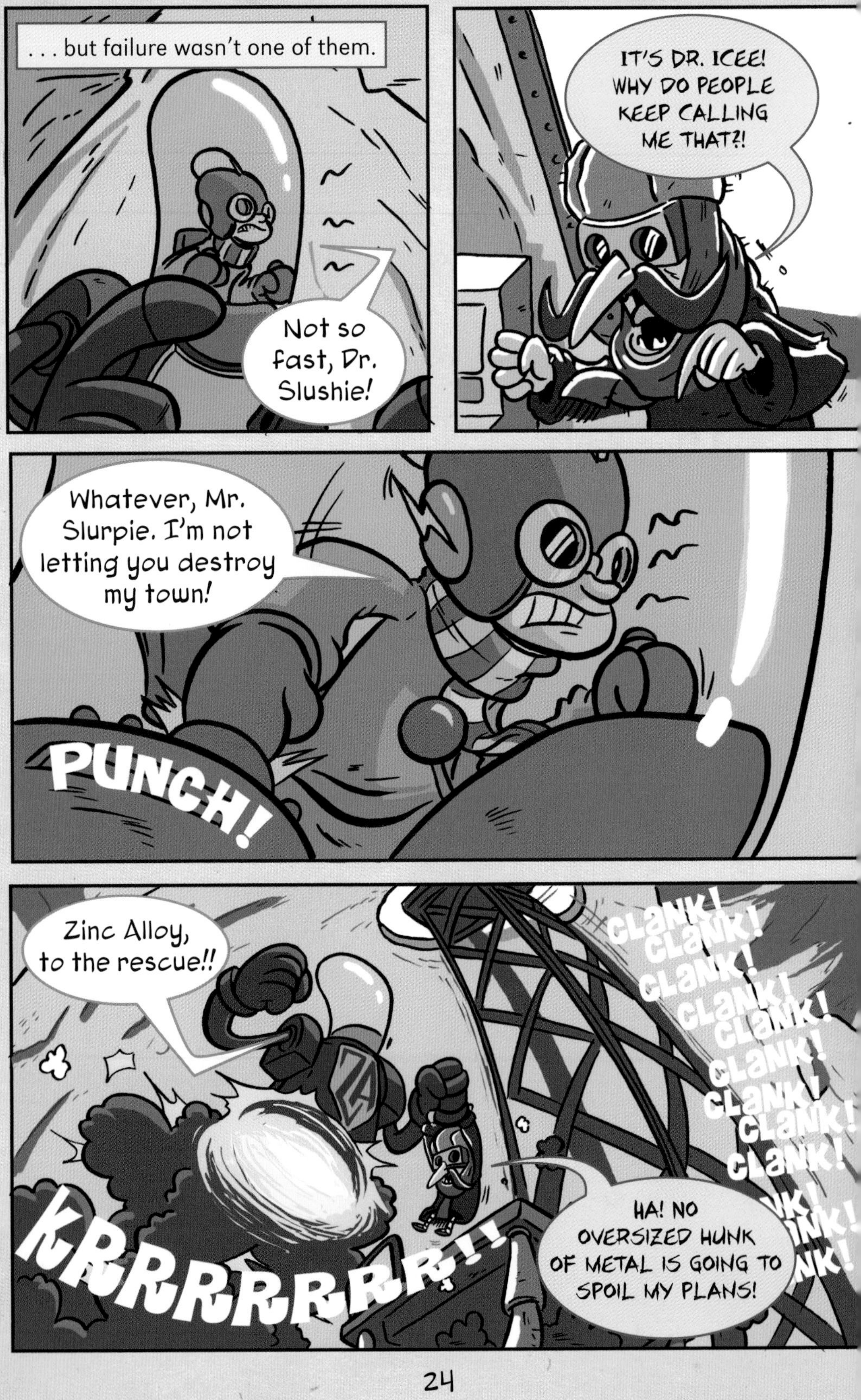

. . . but failure wasn't one of them.
Not so fast, Dr. Slushie!
IT'S DR. ICEE! WHY DO PEOPLE KEEP CALLING ME THAT?!
Whatever, Mr. Slurpie. I'm not letting you destroy my town!
PUNCH!
Zinc Alloy, to the rescue!!
CLANK! CLANK! CLANK! CLANK! CLANK! CLANK! CLANK! CLANK! CLANK!
KRRRRRRRR!!
HA! NO OVERSIZED HUNK OF METAL IS GOING TO SPOIL MY PLANS!

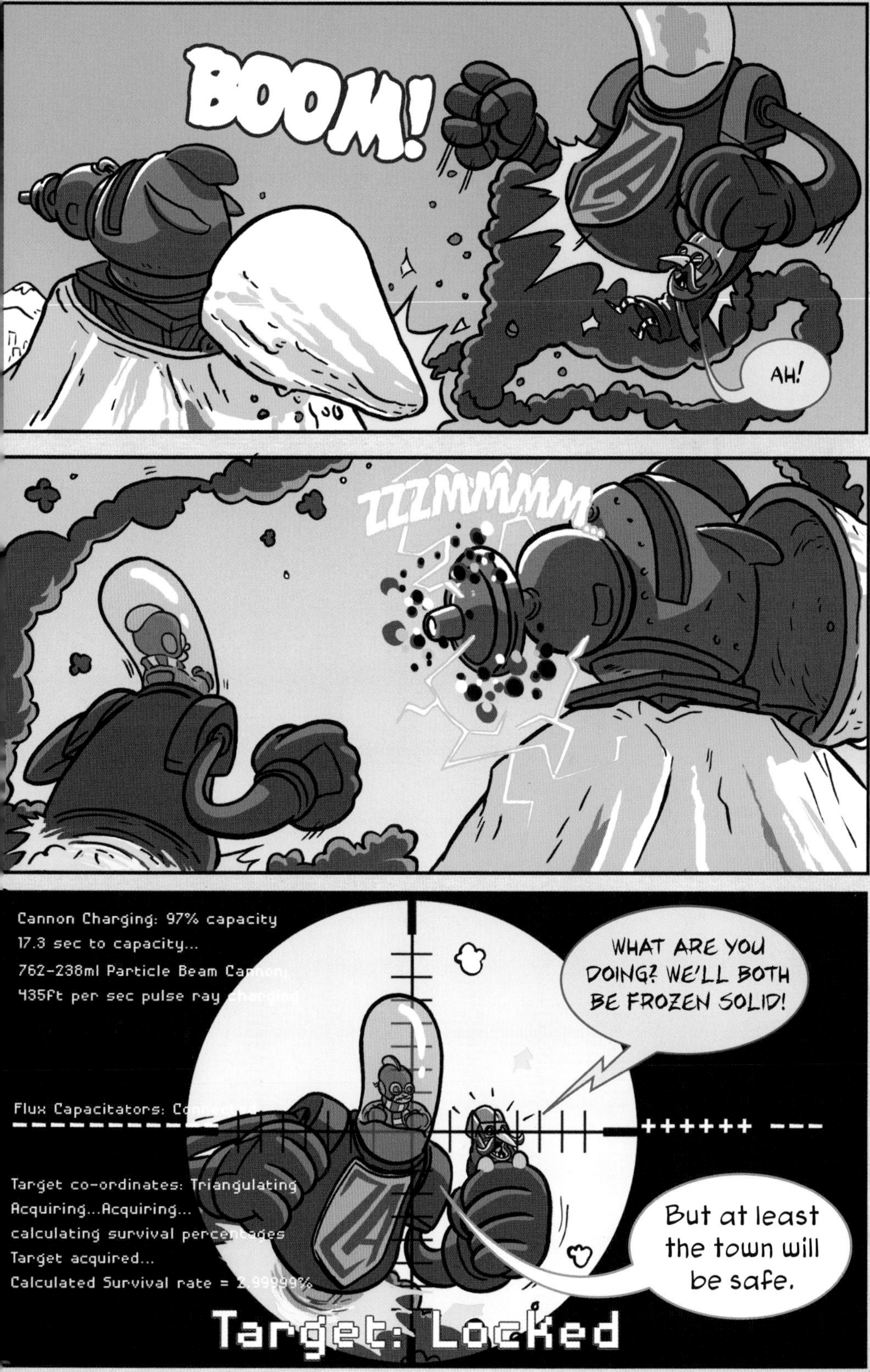
BOOM!
AH!
ZZZMMMMM
Cannon Charging: 97% capacity
17.3 sec to capacity...
762-238ml Particle Beam Cannon,
435ft per sec pulse ray charging
WHAT ARE YOU DOING? WE'LL BOTH BE FROZEN SOLID!
Flux Capacitators: Co
Target co-ordinates: Triangulating
Acquiring...Acquiring...
calculating survival percentages
Target acquired...
Calculated Survival rate = 2.99999%
But at least the town will be safe.
Target: Locked

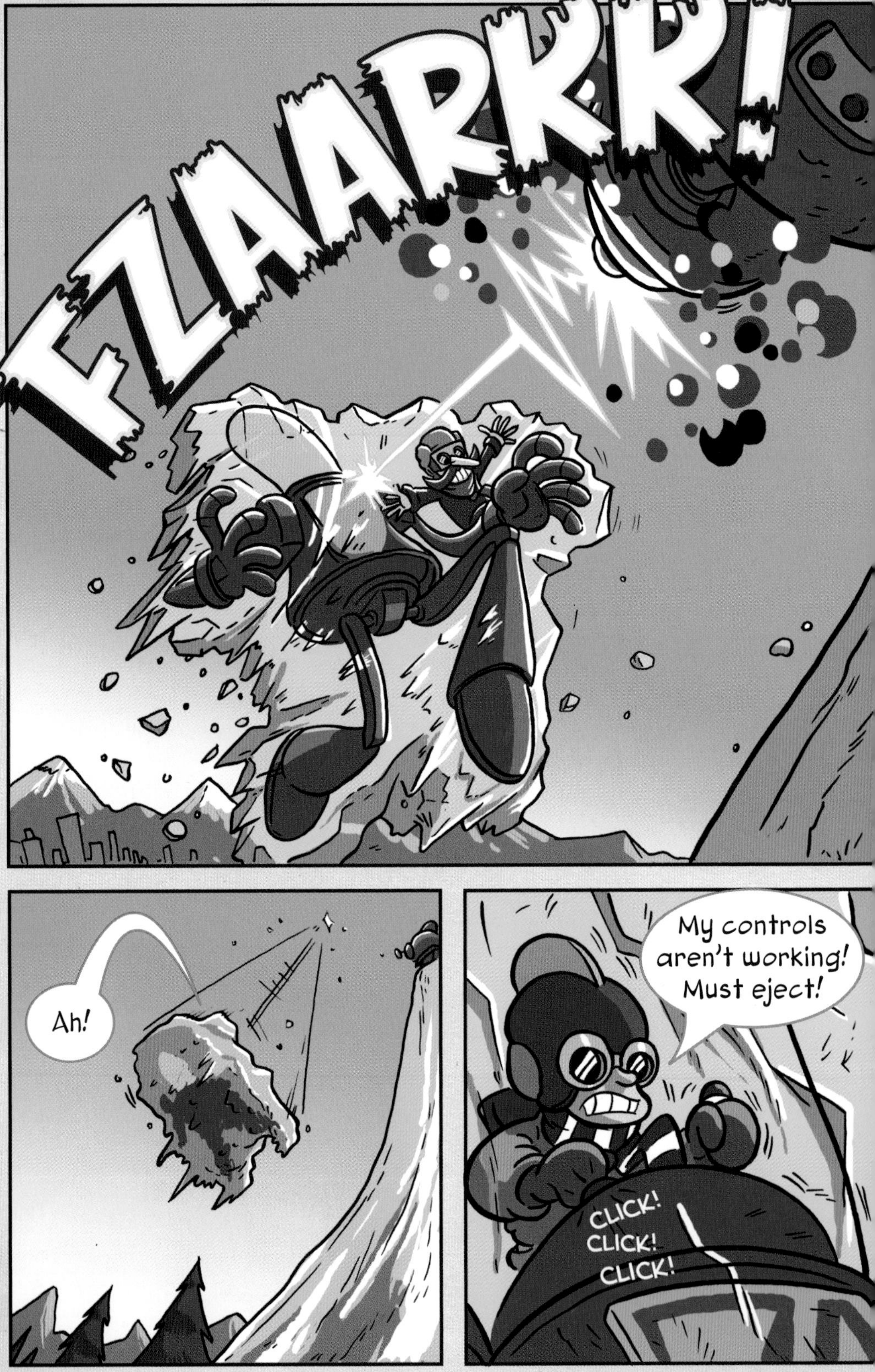
FZAARKK!
Ah!
My controls aren't working! Must eject!
CLICK!
CLICK!
CLICK!

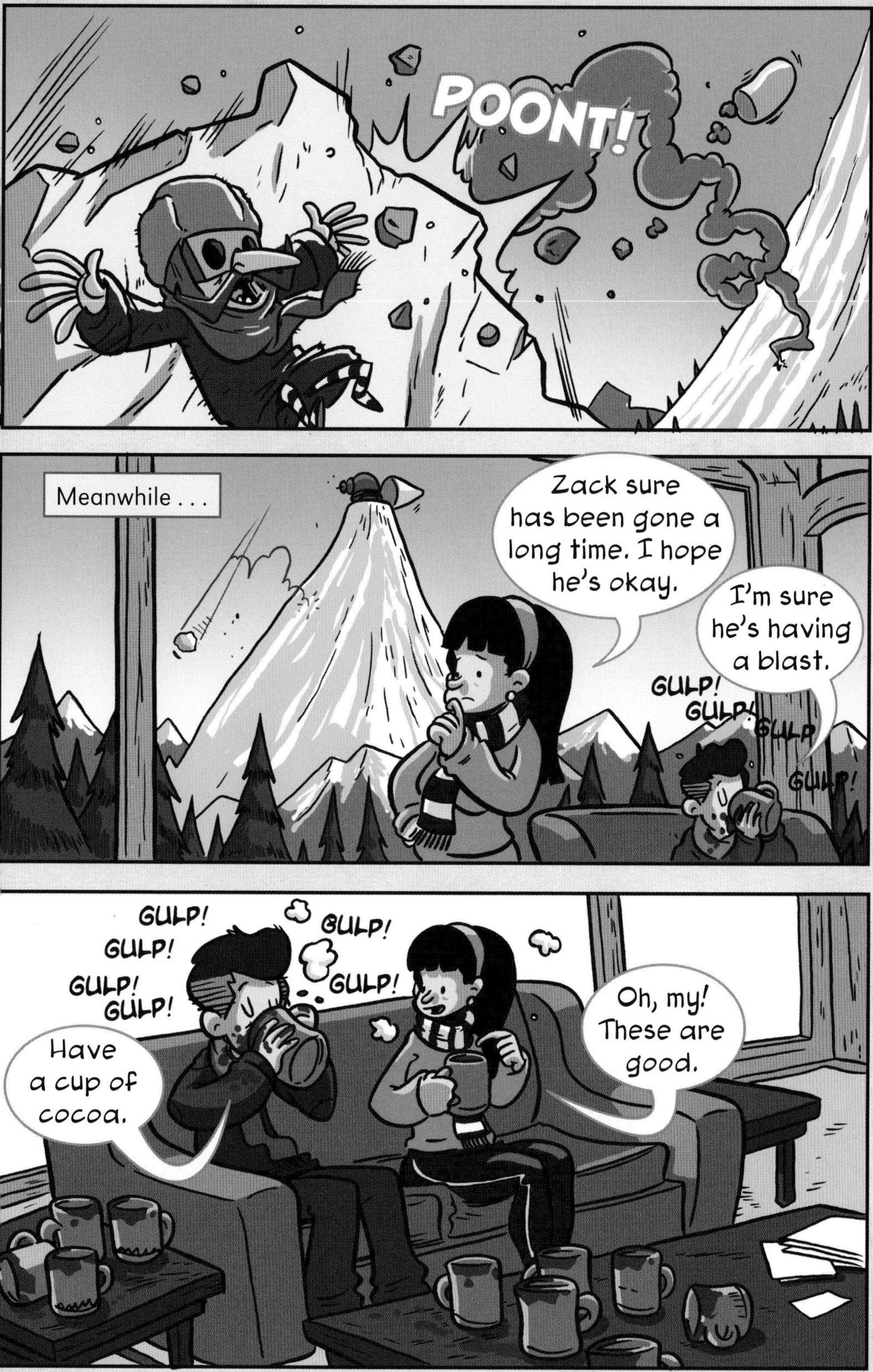
POONT!
Meanwhile . . .
Zack sure has been gone a long time. I hope he's okay.
I'm sure he's having a blast.
GULP!
GULP!
GULP!
GULP!
GULP!
GULP!
GULP!
GULP!
GULP!
GULP!
Have a cup of cocoa.
Oh, my! These are good.

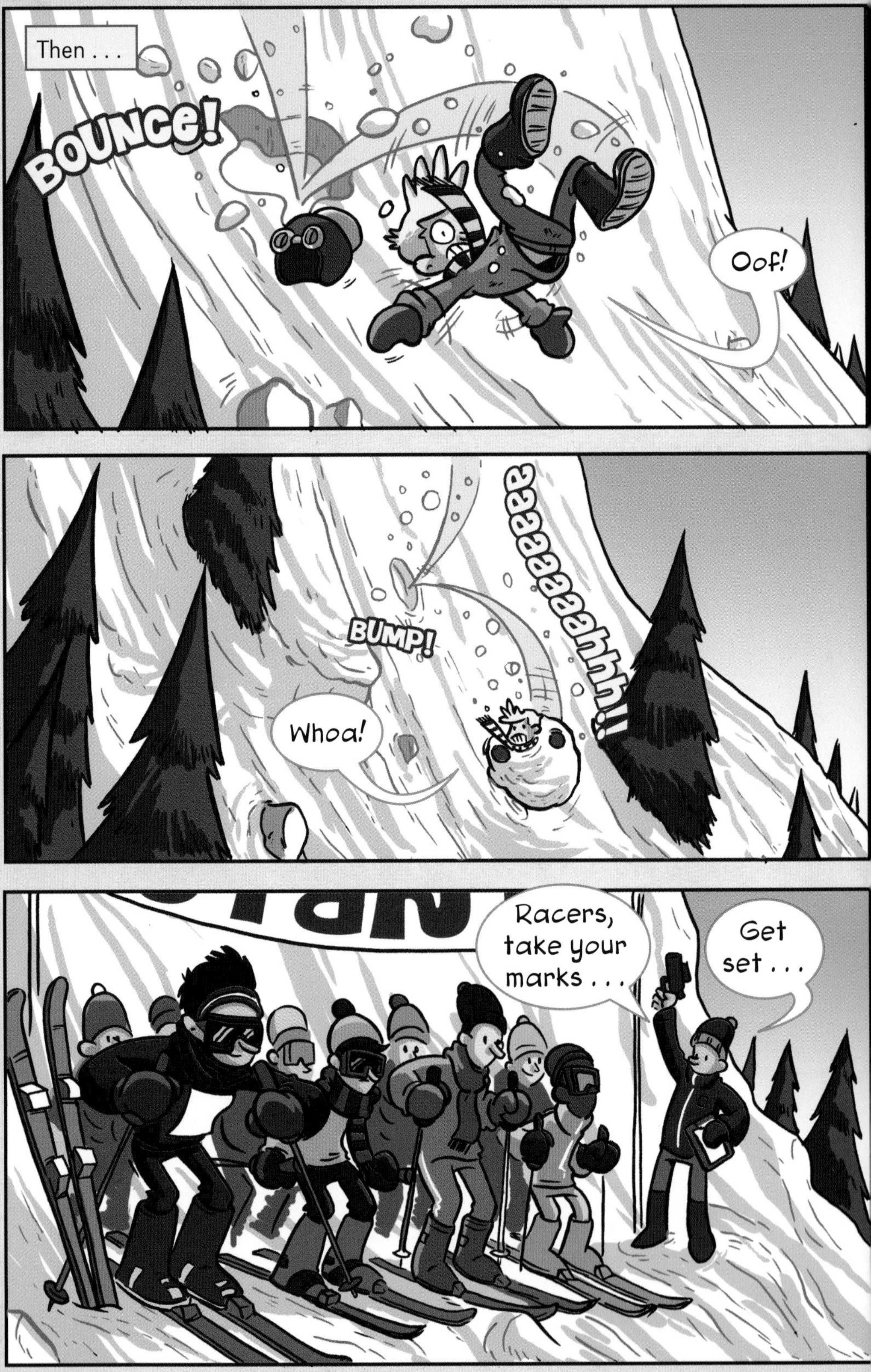
Then . . .
BOUNCE!
Oof!
BUMP!
aaaaaaaaahhhh!!
Whoa!
Racers, take your marks . . .
Get set . . .

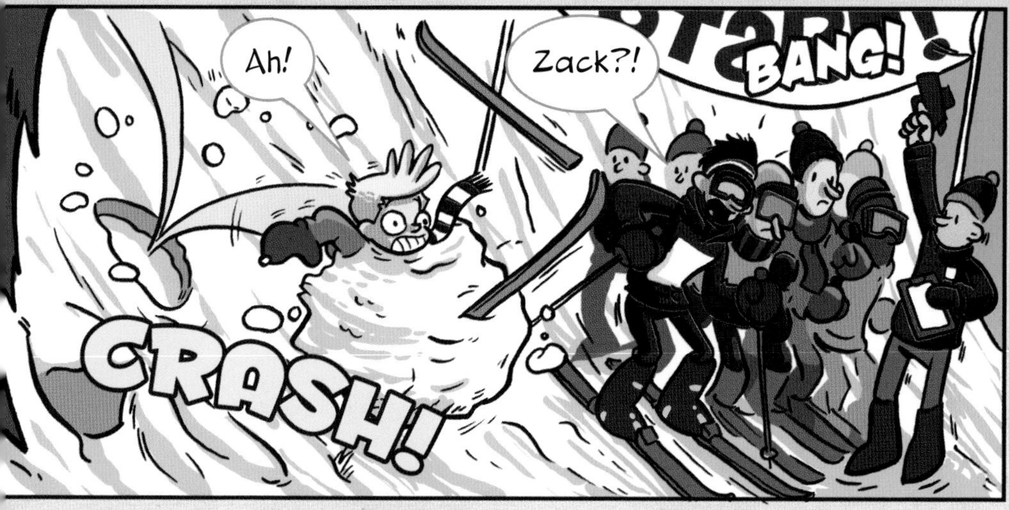
Ah!
Zack?!
BANG!
CRASH!

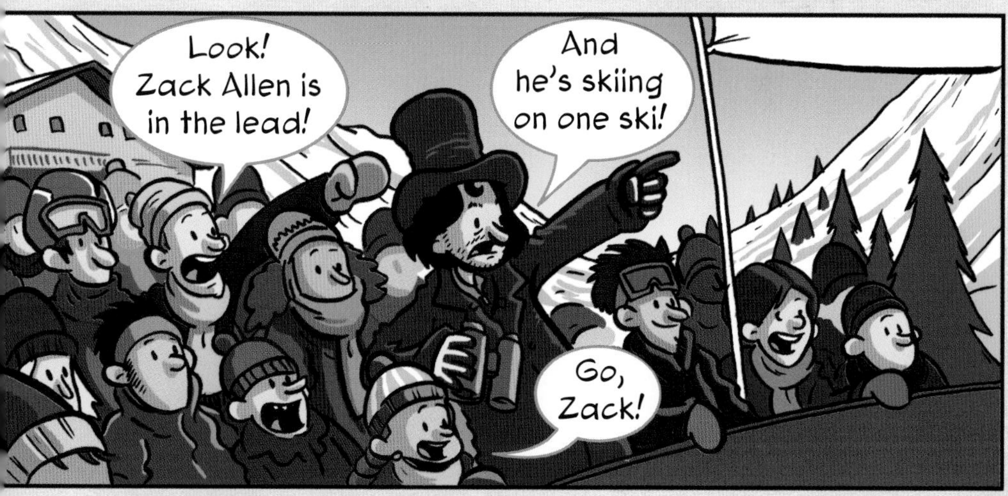
Look! Zack Allen is in the lead!
And he's skiing on one ski!
Go, Zack!

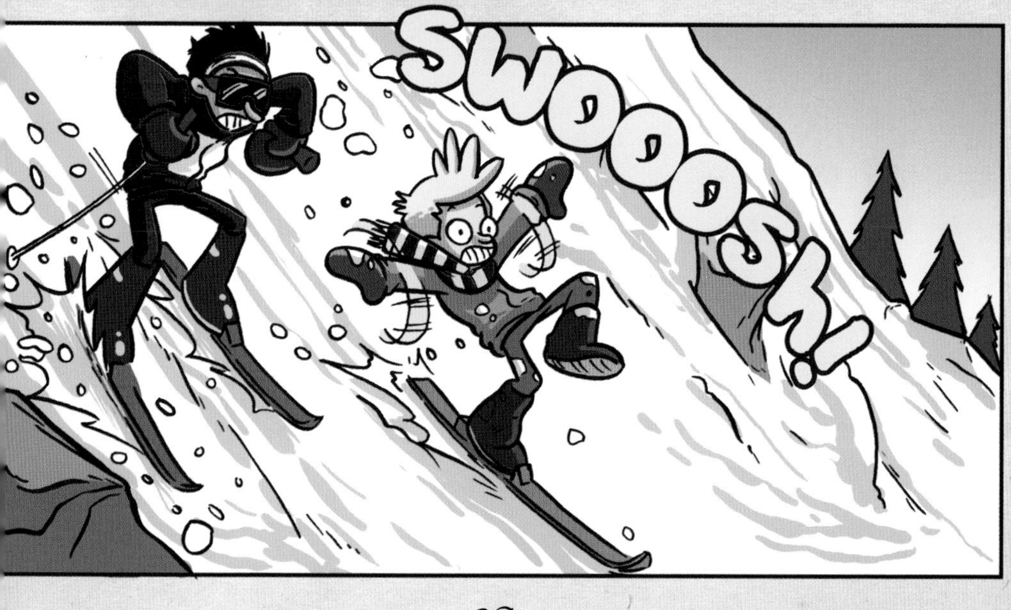
SWOOOOSH!

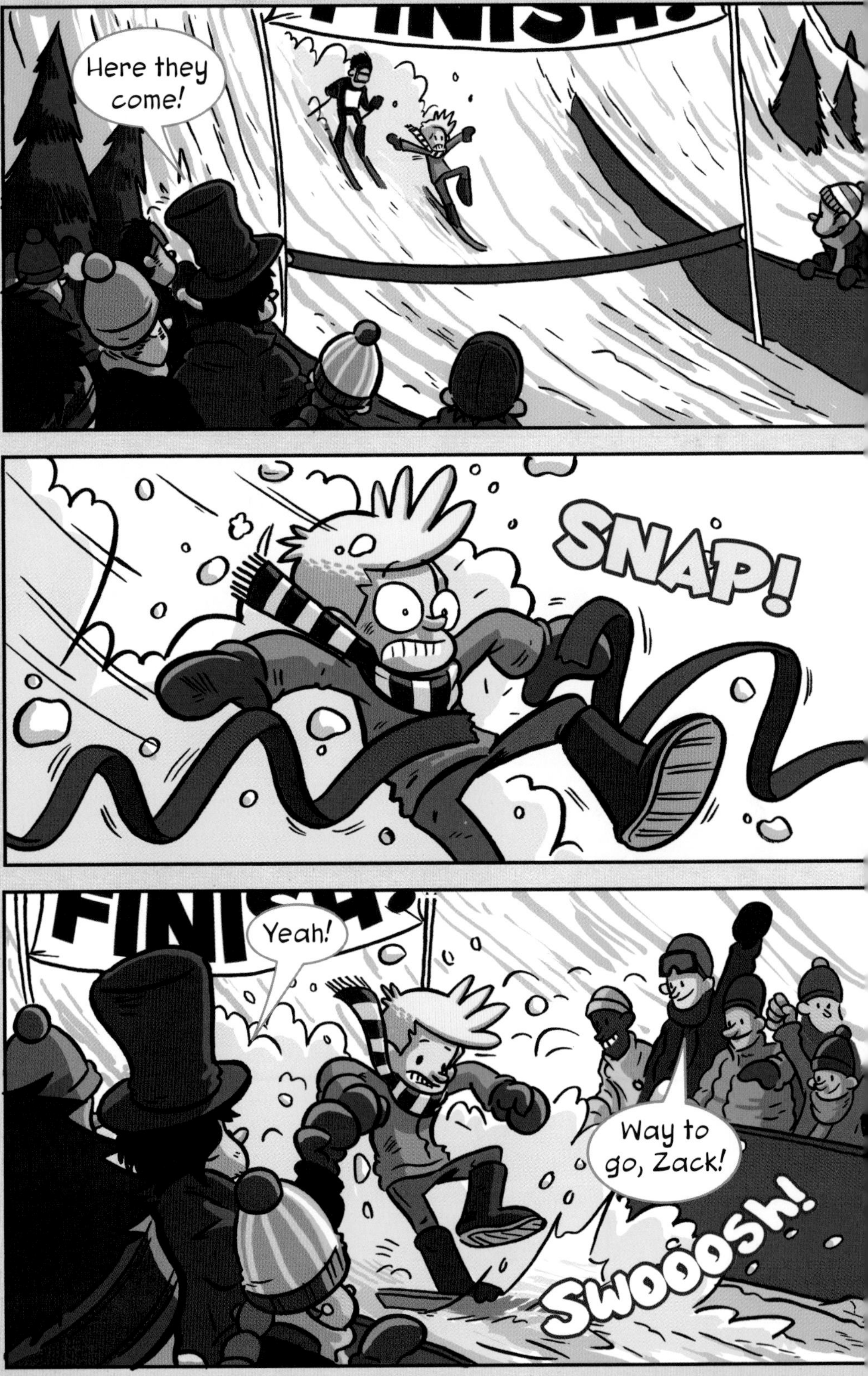
FINISH!
Here they come!
SNAP!
FINISH!
Yeah!
Way to go, Zack!
SWOOOSH!

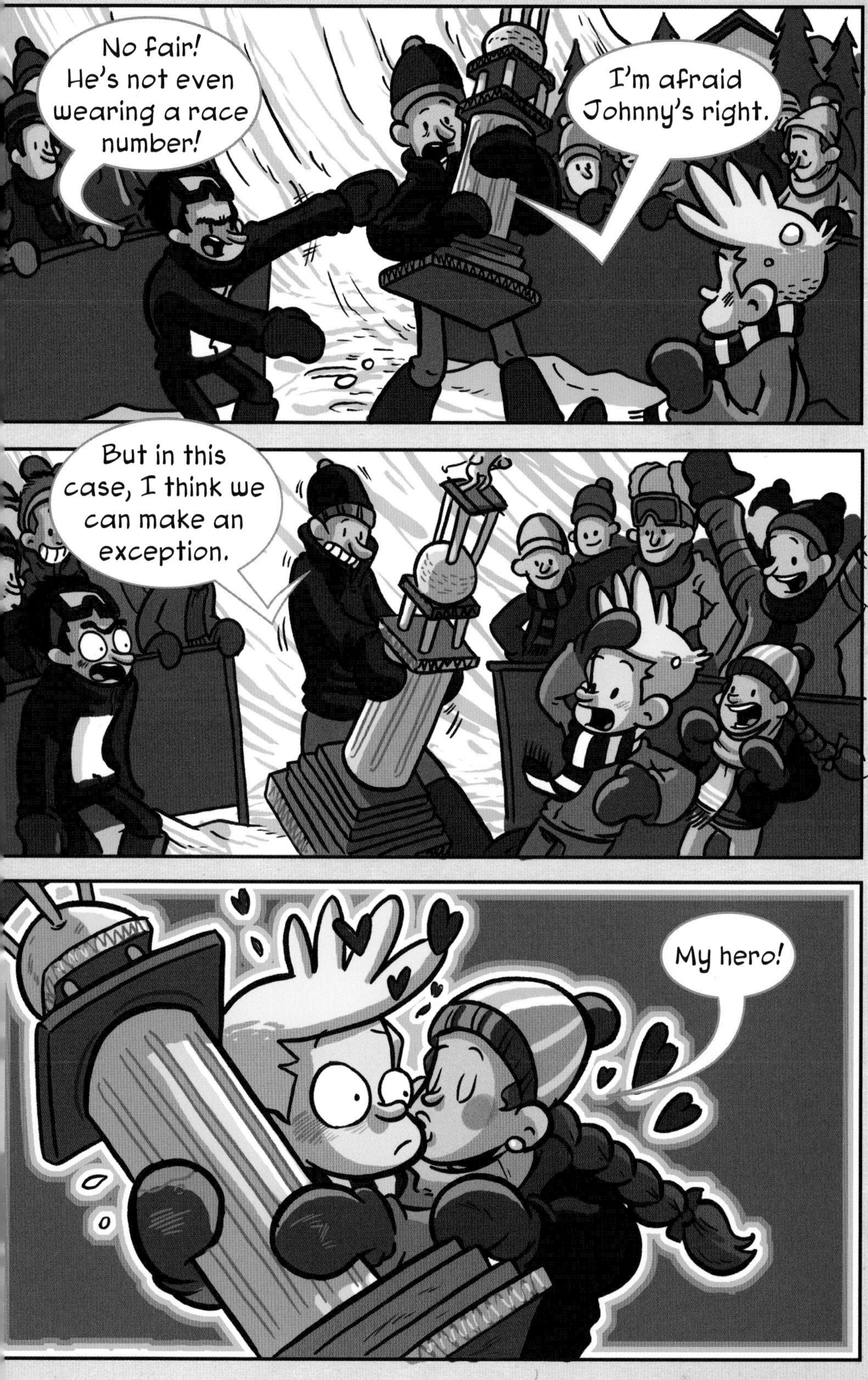
No fair! He's not even wearing a race number!
I'm afraid Johnny's right.
But in this case, I think we can make an exception.
My hero!

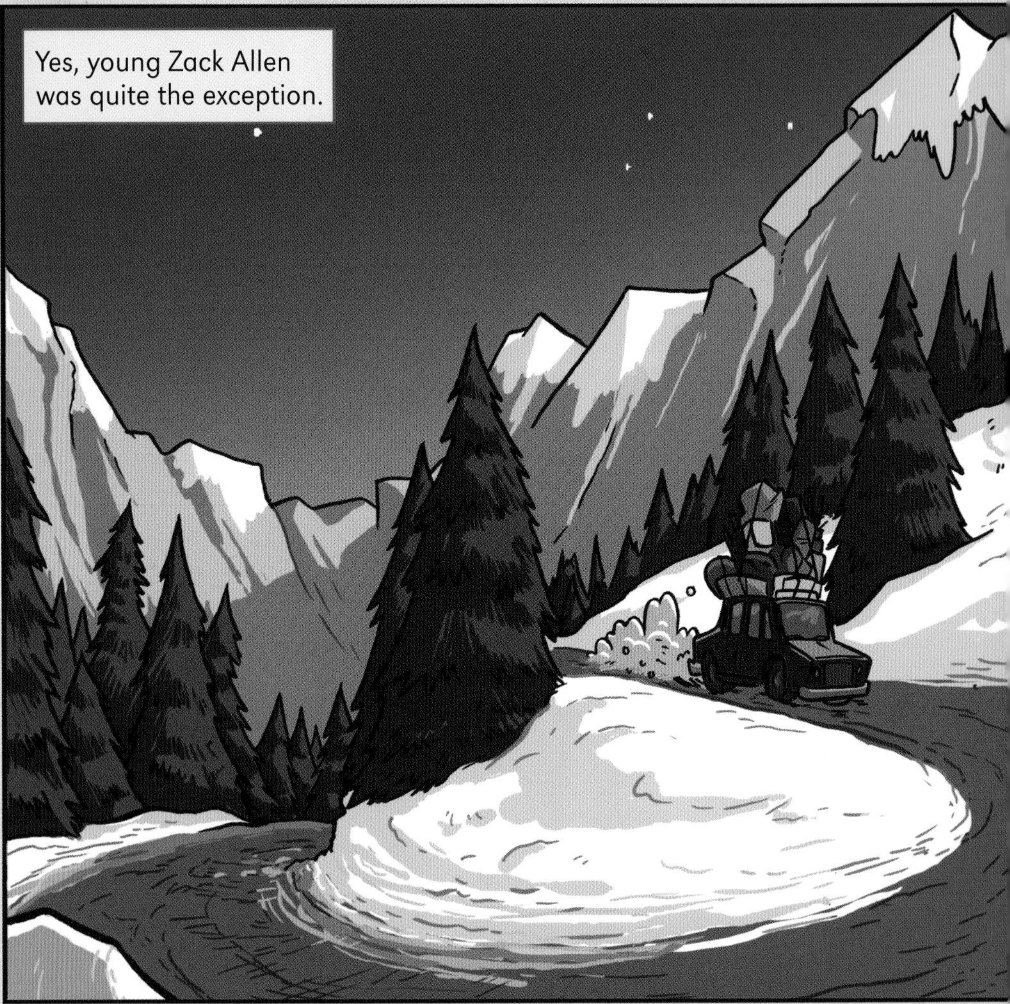
Yes, young Zack Allen was quite the exception.

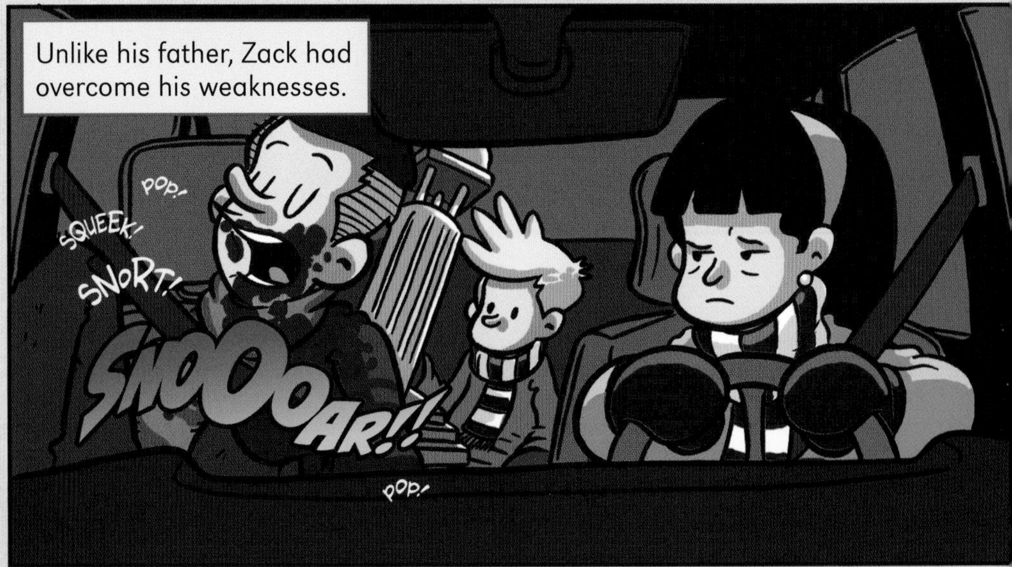
Unlike his father, Zack had overcome his weaknesses.
POP!
SQUEEK!
SNORT!
SNOOOOAR!!
POP!

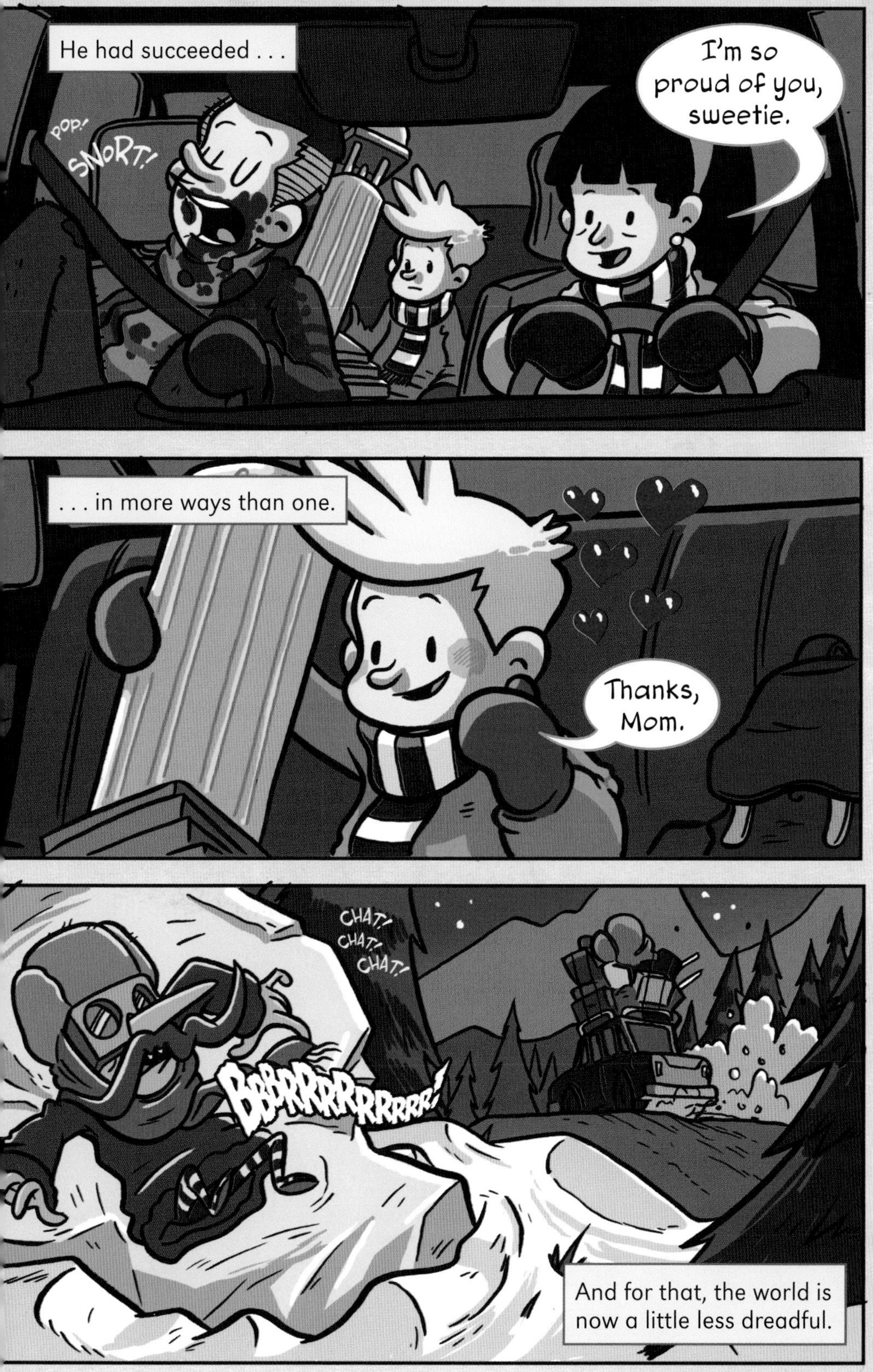
He had succeeded . . .
I'm so proud of you, sweetie.
POP!
SNORT!
. . . in more ways than one.
Thanks, Mom.
CHAT!
CHAT!
CHAT!
BBBRRRRRRRRR!
And for that, the world is now a little less dreadful.

Zinc ALLOY

SUPERHERO SPECS

Zack Allen is just a regular kid. Well, except that he built a totally indestructible robo-suit in his bedroom. But every kid needs some bully protection, right? Here's a look at Zack's all-time greatest gadgets — created to save the world and make the lunchroom a safer place.

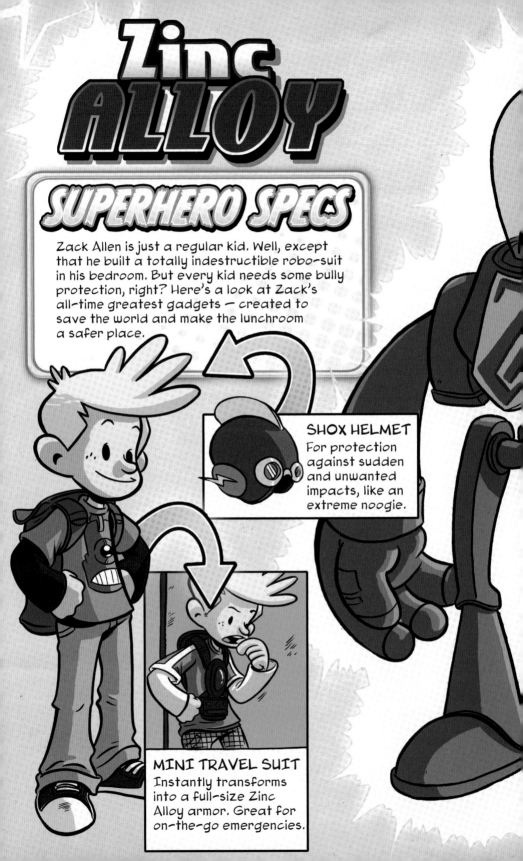

SHOX HELMET
For protection against sudden and unwanted impacts, like an extreme noogie.

MINI TRAVEL SUIT
Instantly transforms into a full-size Zinc Alloy armor. Great for on-the-go emergencies.

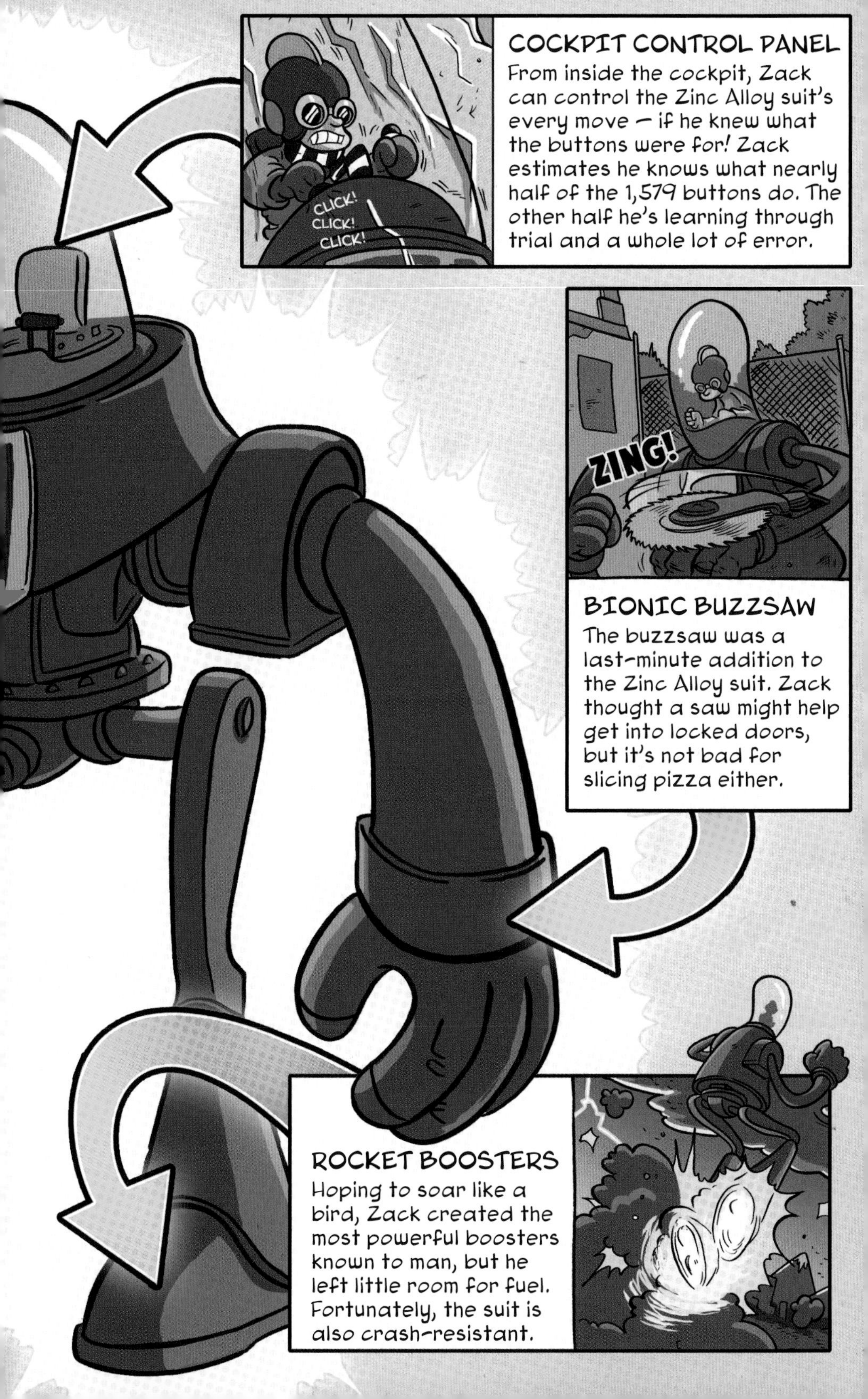
CLICK!
CLICK!
CLICK!
COCKPIT CONTROL PANEL
From inside the cockpit, Zack can control the Zinc Alloy suit's every move — if he knew what the buttons were for! Zack estimates he knows what nearly half of the 1,579 buttons do. The other half he's learning through trial and a whole lot of error.
ZING!
BIONIC BUZZSAW
The buzzsaw was a last-minute addition to the Zinc Alloy suit. Zack thought a saw might help get into locked doors, but it's not bad for slicing pizza either.
ROCKET BOOSTERS
Hoping to soar like a bird, Zack created the most powerful boosters known to man, but he left little room for fuel. Fortunately, the suit is also crash-resistant.

About the Author

Donald Lemke works as a children's book editor. He is the author of the Zinc Alloy graphic novel adventure series. He also wrote *Captured Off Guard*, a World War II story, and a graphic novelization of *Gulliver's Travels*, both of which were selected by the Junior Library Guild.

About the Illustrator

Douglas Holgate is a freelance illustrator from Melbourne, Australia. His work has been published all around the world by Random House, Simon and Schuster, the *New Yorker* magazine, and Image Comics. His award-winning comic "Laika" appears in the acclaimed comic collection Flight, Volume Two.

Glossary

chalet (shal-AY)—a small, wooden house with a sloping roof, often seen at ski resorts

contestants (kon-TESS-tuhntz)—people who are participating in a competition

convention (kuhn-VEN-shuhn)—a large gathering of people who have similar interests

disturb (diss-TURB)—to interrupt someone when he or she is doing something

dread (DRED)—if you dread something, you know it is coming and are very afraid of it

exception (ek-SEP-shuhn)—something or someone that doesn't fit a certain rule or law

savior (SAYV-yor)—a person who saves or rescues others

stealth (STELTH)—silent and sneaky

Discussion Questions

1. Do you think it's fair that Zack won the race? If you were the judge, would you have given him the trophy?

2. Zack's dad has an addiction to hot chocolate. What's your favorite drink?

3. Do you think Mr. Icee will return? Why or why not?

Writing Prompts

1. Zack has a crush on Monique. Have you ever liked anyone? Why did you like them? Write about your crush.

2. Zack won the skiing competition. Have you ever won a game or a competition? What did you win? How did it make you feel?

3. The Zinc Alloy super-suit gives Zach amazing powers and abilities. Design your own super-suit. What powers does it have? What will you use it to do? Write about it. Then, draw a picture of your new suit.